D 40

D-40

Demco

THE SEARCH
FOR HONOR

A Telegraph Western

THE SEARCH FOR HONOR

•

Judy and Ronald Culp

AVALON BOOKS
NEW YORK

Published by Avalon Books,
an imprint of Thomas Bouregy & Co., Inc.
160 Madison Avenue, New York, NY 10016

Library of Congress Cataloging-in-Publication Data

Culp, Ronald
    The search for honor / Ron and Judy Culp.
        p. cm.   (A telegraph Western)
    ISBN 978-0-8034-7611-0 (hardcover : alk. paper)
1. Sheriffs—Fiction.   2. Colorado—Fiction.
I. Culp, Judy.   II. Title.
PS3603.U595 S428
813'.6—dc22

                                    2011018916

PRINTED IN THE UNITED STATES OF AMERICA
ON ACID-FREE PAPER
BY RR DONNELLEY, BLOOMSBURG, PENNSYLVANIA

Dedicated to Father James Stone (1922–2009), Judy's dad. He loved the Arkansas River Valley. Jim ministered to the people of Buena Vista, Colorado, from 1992 to 2003. During our many visits we learned to appreciate and enjoy the wonderful stories of the region.

Acknowledgments

For our friends Pastor Sam Hunnicutt and David Lingle, of Hunt, Texas, who gave us insight into a peace officer's mind:

Sam was formerly Sergeant Samuel Hunnicutt, director (1988 to 1993), McAllen Police Department Training Academy, McAllen, Texas.

David Lingle was deputy sheriff in Wichita County, Texas, 1974 to 1975; city police officer in Iowa Park, Texas, in 1976; and chief deputy sheriff for Clay County, Texas, from January 1, 1977 to November 1, 1978. David "went back to cowboying." Many thanks to both for sharing their experiences while upholding the law.

Finally, we want to acknowledge the life of Jane Kirkham, a woman of the West.

Prologue

A crisp autumn breeze washed over the thriving Colorado mountain community of Buena Vista. The people of the area knew it signaled the beginning of winter. Leaving his comfortable office in the courthouse at Main and Court Street not far from the Arkansas River, Sheriff Oliver Purdy made his way up Main Street. He could almost smell the apple pies the local ladies baked for him as autumn lengthened into the cold of winter. Being a bachelor was a wonderful thing sometimes, and all the widows in town knew that apple pie was his favorite. Raising his hat to the ladies and greeting men along the way with a firm handshake and jovial "Howdy," he stopped to pass some time at the barbershop. He got a shoeshine. Rising from the shine chair, Purdy hitched up his trousers, rolled his shoulders under his suit coat, shot his cuffs to reveal cuff links that were set with large gold nuggets, then generously tipped the shine boy a dime.

Continuing his walk up the street, he cast a hard look at a couple of shifty-eyed men outside one of the shadier of the town's saloons. Thirty-six taverns served the town's adult male population of about fifteen hundred. Some of the high-class saloons boasted imported teak bars, mirrors, and oil paintings and priced everything accordingly. The worst saloons were the take-your-chance tent operations consisting of a canvas tarp and a couple of planks laid across two whiskey barrels, where prices were cheap and the liquor a bare cut above snake-head poison. The rest of the drinking establishments fell somewhere in between. Purdy watched with satisfaction when those fellows slunk through the batwing doors to escape his

1

notice. The chief of the town's force of two policemen happened to also be a whiskey-sodden drunk next to useless in his duties. Tomorrow Purdy would knock some sense into the fellow.

If he were the kind of man to give the matter any thought, Purdy would have chuckled at the irony of the town's three little churches vainly struggling to offset the moral impact of so many saloons on the citizenry. But morals were not his concern. He walked as if he owned the town, for in a way he did. It was in *his* county.

He was a big man, well dressed in a dark suit with a starched and ironed white collar and black string tie, fresh linens a point of pride with him. He was not fat, as some thought at first glance. Anyone who took a second look saw a man heavily muscled through the shoulders and arms, with thick wrists and big hands. Lately, though, he'd had to let his belt out a notch or two. The gout had been bothering him some too. That gout made it more comfortable for Sheriff Purdy to travel around the county on the cushioned seat of a light runabout rig than in the saddle.

A punctual man who kept to a schedule, he knew it would soon be time for his accustomed late-afternoon whiskey or two to whet his appetite before taking supper at what he considered "his" table at Hurley's Restaurant. Not that his appetite ever needed whetting, for he was known as a man who never turned down a meal.

Purdy always had a box seat—gratis, of course, one of the advantages of his job—in the town's three-hundred-seat opera house, and while things remained quiet, he wanted to see Eddie Foy's vaudeville performance before it closed. Besides, tonight he'd been invited to join the widow Esme Rodgers in her curtained "birdcage" box. She was a wealthy woman recently back in town from touring in Europe, and when she walked into a room, every man present turned to look. But, being a diligent man of predictable habits, Purdy would first complete his accustomed walk around the town, his way of making his presence known to all.

He was the first county sheriff elected to the office since

Buena Vista became the county seat. In 1880, when Lake County was divided to form Chaffee County, the residents voted on whether the courthouse should be located in tiny Granite or booming Buena Vista. As it happened, Buena Vista won, but Granite protested because the twelve hundred or so votes cast exceeded the number of permanent legal residents of Buena Vista, even including the women and children. Granite refused to release the court's official records, so one dark night several men from Buena Vista "borrowed" an idle D&RG locomotive and flatcar, steamed up to Granite, broke into the old courthouse, and brought the safe to Buena Vista. The former sheriff, a Granite resident named Jim Peel, held on to the office until the election of 1883, when Purdy won.

Thus Buena Vista transitioned from mining boomtown to a respectable county seat. It became a modern, prosperous little town with many amenities to make life easier. Oddly, a linguistic quirk caused residents to quaintly refer to their town as "B-yunie," in the same way they referred to the old town of Pueblo on the plains east of the mountains as "P-yeblo." Still, they were proud of their town.

The previous year a company in Leadville had installed a Hendley and Meyer eighty-horsepower steam-driven turbine. Turning night into day along that town's Harrison Avenue prompted a clamor from many businesses and even private homes for their own electric lights.

Envious Buena Vistans, not to be outdone, set about organizing their own company to put up a small dam for water-powered dynamos on the Arkansas River at the eastern end of Main Street. The local folks would have electric lights on the streets and even in their houses and businesses if they wanted. Buena Vista grew, prospered, and was jealously regarded up and down the river as putting on airs. Purdy enjoyed a comfortable life.

Approaching the West Main Street railroad crossing, he squinted into a brilliant setting sun low on the mountain skyline to the west. On the other side of the street he saw the Denver & Rio Grande Railroad station's platform now empty, the armed guards gone home for supper. The twenty or so waist-high stacks of silver ingots, fifty-five to a stack, brought from the smelter earlier in the day were already heading east through the mountains on the afternoon train. That marked the first leg of their journey to the Denver Mint.

Four mining districts located in the mountains surrounding Buena Vista produced vast amounts of ore for the smelter in town and the one downriver at Salida. Attracted by the mines, two railroads served the town, moving people as well as tons of freight and mining machinery into and precious metals out from the valley. The D&RG shared its tracks through an agreement with the Denver, South Park & Pacific Railroad, and the tracks bisected the town. Making his way across those tracks, Purdy stepped carefully so as to not scuff the shine on his boots.

Reaching the other side, he headed toward the First Carbonate National Bank, glancing up at the three-sided clock recently installed on a wrought-iron frame above the bank's front door. He paused, then pulled his brand-new Waltham pocket watch from his vest to see if it was keeping correct time. As if acknowledging him, the bank clock's musical chimes rang out a quarter past four. Purdy nodded in satisfaction.

The bank itself was a two-story structure of locally made red brick trimmed with formed-cement framing around its doors and windows. A banner stone proclaimed that the building had been erected in 1883. A disastrous fire had destroyed most of the wooden buildings that once stood on that block. Since it was near closing time at the bank, Purdy decided to show his face. The streets were quiet, the few townspeople who were on the sidewalks heading home in the chilly, early-autumn air. Even the saloons were quiet. Purdy liked that.

Purdy climbed the two steps at the bank's single front door and stepped inside. A customer stood at one of the teller windows, while another man, holding a Gladstone bag, stood by the manager's desk. The massive Hall time-lock safe door stood open. The manager caught Purdy's eye and almost imperceptibly nodded at the man before him. That's when Purdy noticed that the "customers" wore long linen dusters, and bandannas hid their faces. *Robbers!* A surprised Purdy pulled back his coattail, moving his hand to the butt of his sidearm.

"Don't!" one of the men ordered, turning to reveal a sawed-off shotgun pointed at Purdy.

"Hold on," Purdy said. "Don't do nothin' sudden." His heart beat faster. Louder too. Sweat beaded his forehead. His breathing quickened.

"It's a stickup, Sheriff!" the teller cried.

The shotgun-wielding bandit smashed the teller's jaw with the butt of his gun to silence any further outcry.

Purdy's hand rose to his collar. Suddenly he felt as if a huge weight lay on his chest. Had he been shot? A wave of dizziness overcame him, bringing nausea. Purdy's other hand clawed at his tie in a vain effort to loosen it and relieve a choking tightness. Awful pain, like none he'd ever felt, washed over him. Had someone hit him? His legs gave way, and he collapsed on the floor, laboring to breathe.

One of the robbers knelt beside him, loosening his collar for him. "Easy there, Sheriff."

Purdy's eyes fluttered open and fixed on the face above him, which was covered below by a bandanna and above by a floppy hat, so that only the robber's eyes were exposed. "I know you . . . I . . ." He gasped once more, his eyelids drooped, and with a shuddering last breath, he died.

The two holdup men herded the manager and tellers into the broom closet and secured the door by placing a straight-backed chair under the knob. Quickly lowering the window shades, they turned the CLOSED sign in the window at the front door outward and pulled down that shade as well. One of them left the building, walking slowly so as not to attract attention, and made his way around to the east side of the building, where their horses were tied. The remaining robber took a single red carnation from the money-filled Gladstone, stepped around Oliver Purdy's body, and placed the flower on the manager's desk before following the other man outside. No one took any notice of the pair as they mounted their horses and rode out of town at a walk.

Chapter One

Tilman Wagner uttered an oath and shook the pages of the *Leadville Chronicle*. He had been reading a news item about an unfortunate miner whose age-stiffened fingers had caused him to mishandle a capped stick of Giant Powder and blow himself into eternity.

"'Up in years,' they say the man was," he grumbled out loud. "'More than forty years old.' Forty. Hah. That's not old! According to that, I ought to have one foot in my grave. Who's the imbecile who wrote this? Some young dandy of a reporter from back East," he guessed.

"Tilman? Are you talking to someone out there on the porch?" His wife, Catherine, stood just inside the door to the house. "I don't see a soul. Besides, you don't have a foot in the grave at all. In fact, you have a boisterous set of twin babies in here to lay false to that statement. Don't you?" She laughed as her husband hemmed and hawed and blushed, his face bright red but his shoulders straightening out a notch.

Out on the nearby Cottonwood Pass road a buckboard slowed and turned into the drive leading up to the Wagners' two-story wood-frame house. "That's him. That's Tilman Wagner there on the front porch," the driver, Chaffee County Commissioner Ray Lewis, said.

"Well, I'm still not sure about this," Lester Page, the passenger and also a commissioner, said.

"Listen, now's not the time to back down. The majority vote carried. We think this is the right thing to do."

"All right, but I'll tell you again, I've heard talk about Wagner's shooting scrapes down in Texas even before the

Ward killing here in town. Why," Page said, his voice rising in pitch as it always did when he got excited, "his own son, James Wagner, told my boy stories about gunplay down in New Mexico! We don't know how many other shootings Tilman Wagner's done. I ask you, what kind of man takes a young'un chasin' rustlers? I'll tell you. A killer does!"

"Les, don't talk like that," Lewis said. "You just get all agitated. Nobody expected Oliver Purdy to die. Just you remember, we're only asking Wagner to stand in as sheriff until after the election can be done. Besides, I know for a fact he never shot that Bill Ward fellow—a Mex bounty hunter done it. Happened right after I come here to the Valley from Pueblo. Wagner's been a solid citizen—even married a local gal, didn't he?"

"I know when I'm beat. Still, don't you forget, I voted against Wagner. No matter what you or anybody else says, to my mind the man's a killer, and somebody's gonna get hurt."

Tilman Wagner folded the newspaper and disgustedly threw it onto the wicker table beside his rocking chair, rising to greet his visitors. In his stocking feet he stood over six feet tall. Suspenders held up his dark blue trousers, and he wore a white shirt with no collar. Gray eyes squinted in the bright afternoon sunlight, the thin line of his mouth turning down as he recognized the two men in the buckboard. Over his shoulder he announced to his wife, "Company." He heard the screen door squeak as she came back onto the porch to stand beside him.

When the light wagon halted by the cast-iron hitching post at the foot of the walk, Wagner, hands jammed in his pockets, leaned against one of the porch posts. "Light an' set, boys," he called. "First time I've ever known you to come out here, so I expect this is county business and not a social call."

"You're right, Mr. Wagner," Ray Lewis said, tipping his bowler to Catherine. "Miz Wagner." He looked at Tilman. "It's business. We've got a proposition for you, and it won't take up much of your time." Neither man accepted the offer to get out of the buckboard.

"Do tell," Wagner answered, fixing his eyes on the slightly built little man scowling at him from the passenger seat of the wagon. "Howdy, Page." Easy to see what Lester Page thought of him. Tilman shrugged. Not his concern.

"Wagner."

Lewis spoke up. "Wagner, I guess you've heard about what happened to Sheriff Purdy."

"I have. Word of something like that gets around town pretty quick."

"You know his deputy quit last month and ran off to Pueblo to get married?"

"I haven't seen him around. Didn't know why. What are you getting at, Lewis?"

"We need to elect a new sheriff, but it'll take a while to get everything in order. Purdy's the only sheriff the county has ever had." Lewis continued, "We'd like you to take the job as Chaffee County Sheriff. It's not permanent, you understand. You'll be the interim sheriff until Purdy's term expires next year."

"It pays seventy-five dollars a month," Page volunteered, "what you Texas boys like to call 'gun wages.'"

"Shut up, Page," Lewis snapped.

Wagner shoved away from the post and strode down the porch steps quickly to stand beside the wagon. He leaned in close to Page, so close that the man shrank back. "I ain't shot a man in ages," he hissed, causing Lester Page to recoil even farther and bump against Lewis' shoulder. "Strappin' on my six-gun again might get my blood up, though."

Lewis scowled, pushing Page away. "The commissioners voted to offer the job to you. The mayor agrees you're good for the job. Maybe you can find them that robbed the bank. What do you say?"

"Did you ask anybody else?"

"Some of us wanted to offer the job to Jim Peel, the town marshal at Granite," Page blurted. "He used to be the county sheriff before Purdy won in '83. I bet Peel'd not hesitate to take the job, what with his experience." Page glared back at Tilman.

"Now, Page, why'd you tell him that?" Lewis hadn't wanted to bring Page, but the man had insisted.

"That's all right, Lewis. I met Peel once but can't say I know the gent," Tilman said.

"Well, what do you say, Wagner?"

"Shouldn't I be the deputy sheriff, since I'm hired instead of being elected?"

"We figure since Lawyer Thomas says there's nothing about this kind of situation in the statutes, we're on our own. Take it, and you'd have the full authority of the office."

"That makes sense. Well, it might beat layin' about the house all day. Tell you what. I'll think about it," Wagner said. "Give you my answer tomorrow."

"I look forward to it," Ray Lewis said. Raising his hat, he said, "Miz Wagner." At her answering nod, he shook the reins, startling the dozing horse and making the buckboard take off with a lurch around the curving driveway back toward the road.

Wagner watched the light wagon moving at a fast clip down the road toward town. He chuckled.

"Shame on you, Tilman," Catherine said, "picking on poor Commissioner Page like that."

"Page is a sour little man." Wagner defended himself while draping one long arm across his wife's shoulders, "He's mad at the world for bein' so short that he has to stand on a box behind the counter in his store or else nobody'll see him!"

"And you're God-sent to point that out to him, aren't you?" Catherine dodged Tilman's attempt to steal a kiss and slipped from under the arm. "Are you going to take the job?"

Serious now, Wagner climbed the steps to the porch and resumed his seat in the rocking chair. "Ray Lewis is a good man. So is most of the council. Those bandits are pretty bold to take the bank right in the middle of town the way they did. I'll think about it, and let's you and me talk it over."

A loud wail came from inside the house, soon joined by another, equally loud. "The twins are waking from their naps," she reminded him. From the nursery the babies, a year-old boy and girl, announced their demands for immediate attention. Tilman had converted the room from what he'd always considered his late son, Dan's, bedroom back in the day when a widowed Catherine Stone ran a boardinghouse. "We'll have to talk later," she said, taking his hand and tugging him into the house.

Chapter Two

After supper, with the twins bathed, fed, and in bed, Catherine and Tilman took their coffee in the parlor. There was a tension between them. Neither had mentioned the job offered by the commissioners earlier that day, but both knew it was time to talk.

"You always said you don't believe in coincidences," Catherine began. "Stagecoaches and banks being robbed here and on the road to Granite, poor Sheriff Purdy's heart giving out, and here you're offered the job as high sheriff of Chaffee County."

"Coincidence? I don't get your meaning," Tilman said. He'd been half listening, his mind elsewhere as he considered how he should open the discussion.

"Tilman," she chided, "how soon you forget! Butter's moving back home to Colorado." She unfolded a piece of paper and placed it on the table by Tilman's chair.

MOVING BACK TO COLORADO STOP UNCLE NATHROP
DEAD STOP I AM A LANDOWNER STOP BUTTER

"Oh," Tilman said when he saw the paper. "How could that slip my mind?" Three days before Oliver Purdy died during the bank robbery, a telegram had arrived to announce that Butter Pegram, his wife, Neala, and their four children were moving back to his uncle's ranch south of Buena Vista near the town of Nathrop. In fact, the family should be arriving any day now.

"You two have looked after each other as long as I've known you," Catherine said. "I think you want that job, and you'll

10

need Butter to keep you out of trouble. As I said, no coincidence!"

"As usual you're right, Catherine," Tilman admitted, relief evident in his voice. "I do want to take it. But I've never been a sheriff, and I'm not sure I've got what it takes."

"Dear, the commissioners asked you because they know you are an honorable man. They respect you."

"Maybe they've forgotten how I was when I first came here." He paused. "Lester Page sure seems to remember. He kept waiting for me to pull out my gun, I think."

"You've changed. With God's help, Pastor Fry and I saw to that! Except you're like an old fire horse put out to pasture yet missing the excitement," Catherine said patiently. "You hear the alarm, and you're ready to head for the smell of smoke."

"You two ganged up on me—"

Catherine started to interrupt, but her husband wouldn't allow it.

"I know, I know," Tilman said. "You're right. But seriously, I wonder if I'm not too old for this, Catherine." It was never Cat or Cate, for Tilman always called her by her full given name. "What does Lewis really expect me to do?" Tilman rose from his chair to pace the parlor floor.

"I'm not the youngster who came up here bent on killin' somebody after Dan was murdered, always in the saddle or hanging around saloons looking for information. Then I met you. Why, I was scared of marrying again, and you knew it. So I went a-hellin' around Texas to help John Law get Lomida and that new wife of his, Miss Maddie, away from those border-jumpers down at the Rio Grande. When they were safe, I had to come back to you."

"Yes, Tilman, that's all true, but you've settled, and those days are behind you now," she countered. "You'll be sheriff only until Purdy's term runs out. Those men know that you're honest, and they also know you can't be bought off. Oliver Purdy seemed a decent man, but he was on 'Smiley' Charbonneau's payroll since he took office. Honor was not exactly his strong suit." She smiled as her husband looked at her in surprise. "Everybody knew that. Don't look so surprised. Pastor

Fry tells me that very little in this county went on without the sheriff's knowledge and approval."

"That's how some sheriffs retire rich," Tilman said with a laugh. "I've seen it in a lot of places. They have their hands in things going on around the courthouse. They're real friendly with shyster lawyers and politicians, and they get paid off to make sure things go right for certain people. Folks who cross a sheriff like that, a man who runs roughshod over everybody, get busted up and land in jail. But I don't hold with that way of doing things. I believe an honest man can make sure things are done according to the law and not by shady backroom deals with whoever has the fattest wallet."

"I know you'll stand for what you believe in, Tilman," she said. "You always have. Others know that as well. That's why you're being asked."

"But, truth to tell"—Tilman groped for the words—"sometimes when it's cold here, and the snow drifts belly-deep to my horse, I have more aches and pains than I used to. There's always the chance of gunplay, and I don't move as fast as I did. . . ."

"Tilman," Catherine said. "Stop. You're only saying those things because you think they're my worries. They're not. You've never been a duelist. I know you're calm, a planner, and you don't rush into danger. You don't have to convince me."

Tilman returned to his chair, surprise evident on his face. He'd expected resistance from Catherine because she'd made it clear after his and Butter's return from New Mexico Territory that Tilman's six-gun ought to remain in the bottom dresser drawer, and the Winchester rifle on the rack over the back door in case wolves got among the livestock.

Catherine studied her husband. "I've heard you grumble about this latest gang of robbers. You think you're that *somebody* who ought to do *something* before *somebody* gets hurt. Now *somebody has* gotten hurt."

"Catherine, those robbers didn't know that Oliver Purdy would keel over dead. They didn't harm anyone on purpose."

"Maybe not, but who knows what will happen next?"

"I admit, it can be dangerous. I also know, if I don't step in as sheriff, who will? Commissioner Page? Or some down-on-his-luck miner looking for three squares and a bunk? I've traveled some hard trails, and I know how to deal with outlaws."

"Well," Catherine said, "I know this. You've faced as many soiled diapers as you can stand, and I see the look on your face when one of the twins burps sour milk on your shirt. You miss the excitement of going out and doing the things you've always done. I'm not standing in your way. You won't be gone for any long rides—you'll be right here in Chaffee County—and the twins are still at the age where eating and sleeping and crying is all they do. We both know I'll keep busy with a double load of diapers and bottles to wash.

"You'll be home in the evening to watch them walk and help them. And"—she paused—"I'd like to have you here, not gallivanting off for parts unknown after another telegram calls for help. Didn't Butter's telegram say he would be here soon? He can be your deputy, and you'll know your back will be covered. Especially with this gang of robbers out for whatever they can get."

"You're sure you won't mind?" Tilman asked, torn between love for his new family and his sense of adventure.

"Let me make a wee change to a quote from *Hamlet:* 'Methinks he doth protest too much.'" She laughed. Catherine was an avid reader, but Tilman found Shakespeare too hard to follow. That fellow Mark Twain wrote things more to his liking. And Scott's *Ivanhoe,* a tale of right and wrong, was one of Tilman's favorites. "It's settled," she said. "You'll have Butter to keep you safe, and you'll be around in the evenings to watch the twins and help me with them."

"James is sixteen and does a man's work around the ranch. We can handle it." Tilman couldn't help the excitement he felt at the thought of trying to track down the gang that was threatening the place where he and his lived.

"Of course we can." Catherine rejoiced as she saw the new light in Tilman's eye. She knew he loved his family, but she also knew that, like Ivanhoe, he needed to try to right the wrongs of this Earth.

Chapter Three

Prosper Charbonneau, as was his custom, sat in the south-facing bay window of his house near Town Lake off Cotton-wood Avenue in Buena Vista. Bright morning light filled the room as he savored a second steaming cup of coffee; the rich, dark brew was made from beans specially shipped each month from New Orleans. He missed his coffee when traveling, and the trip he'd recently returned from had lasted longer than he'd expected.

He frowned. Hammering and sawing noises from the workers building the Lakeside Hotel interrupted his accustomed peace. He'd have to move up the date for starting the new house; no, it would truly be a mansion. He planned to make his new home one that would show all who saw it that here resided a man of great wealth and importance.

Footsteps sounded on the front porch, followed by the doorbell. He heard voices, and the housekeeper opened the door to his office. "Mr. Sand left a note."

"Give it to me, Charlene," he said. Sand was one of Charbonneau's sources of information around the Valley.

The housekeeper did so and left the room. Charbonneau unfolded the paper and read the hastily scribbled words, *Wagner new shurf*. No details as to when, where, or how. Sand was barely literate, but the man was dependable. Prosper would have to look into this. "Charlene," he called, "have the groom bring the runabout."

As he dressed, he studied his reflection in the mirror. A mixed-ancestry Creole looked back at him. The swarthy complexion and dark eyes set above high cheekbones showed that there had been a person of color in his line, somewhere far back in the past. With the back of his right index finger he knuckled smooth his pencil-thin mustache. As he'd matured, he'd affected an anchor beard, pointed and always neatly trimmed. He liked the devilish look it gave him. He smiled, lips drawn back over his strong, even teeth.

Charbonneau's thoughts returned to the implications of former Sheriff Oliver Purdy's death. Their business dealings had favored them both. More than that, they were the very foundation of Prosper's plans to gain political power and influence in the Valley. Powerful men in Denver knew his name, for his ambition was boundless. He hoped one day to win a seat in the statehouse. But first, business: Tilman Wagner would take Oliver Purdy's place. A sheriff could be a powerful ally, for he worked hand-in-hand with the county attorney, the commissioners' court made up of four precinct judges, and, through them, the county judge. These were the men who ran the county government, and Charbonneau wanted to control them. Two of the four precinct judges accepted "favors," while the current county judge liked to rough up crib girls, so Purdy had made sure the girls left town when the doctor said they were well enough to travel.

When Marie Fleur, Prosper's only daughter, had returned from school in New Orleans, he'd encouraged her to marry the then-Sheriff Jim Peel, so Prosper would have him in his pocket, but he'd had to move quickly when Peel lost the election to Purdy. Things had worked out, though, for Purdy had enjoyed "bonuses," so he'd looked the other way and hadn't interfered with the houses Charbonneau owned and operated in the county's red-light districts. In return, the madams had met regularly with Purdy and pushed envelopes of cash across the table into the big man's hand. It wasn't actually extortion, for the cash—anywhere from twenty-five to one hundred dollars, depending on the clientele frequenting each house—represented fines the towns imposed on the houses.

As sheriff and county tax collector, Purdy had taken a cut and directed the remainder of the money to the different precincts and town councils where the houses were located.

Some of the cash became public funds to be used for civic improvements. That's the way things were done. That was the price of doing business, Charbonneau often joked.

Charbonneau owned gambling tables in half of the town's thirty-odd saloons, respectable enough in the Colorado mining district. The income was steady, for the operators were skilled at cheating. Charbonneau made sure of that. Again, Purdy had taken a cut—small, but it added up over time.

Charbonneau had spent years working his way up from operating independently as a sidewalk bunco-steerer into other rackets up and down the Arkansas River Valley. Unfortunately, his greed and lust for riches had led to mistakes in his early years. Cruelly efficient with a knife, he'd acquired the nickname "Smiley" for the wicked grin he flashed at his victims. Now he made every effort to further distance himself from that past.

He was not the biggest dog in the fight for supremacy among those who preyed on the weak or corrupt, and neither was he the smartest, so he made up for those deficiencies by being more cunning and dangerous than most. Tens of thousands of dollars had come his way, and he had every reason to expect that flow to continue. Learning to distance himself from the day-to-day operation of most of his "business interests," he'd made sure that no one could implicate him directly in any unsavory or unlawful activity without peeling away many skillfully imposed protective layers. He paid a lot of money to several attorneys to make it so. It cut down on the danger that way. It also protected his reputation as a solid citizen.

"The runabout is here, sir," Charlene announced from the door.

With a final tug to tighten the knot in his colonel's tie and make sure the ends hung evenly, he was ready to go. Time to pay a visit to the hotel and find out the latest on the new man. Tilman Wagner held a decent reputation and appeared to be honest. But all men had a price. Prosper just had to find out what Wagner wanted. He should meet with the new sheriff to see which direction the man favored. Best be the right direction, for Charbonneau didn't want his plans disturbed by a two-bit sheriff. Especially by one who was not even a real sheriff.

Chapter Four

Tilman glanced down at the badge pinned to his vest. *Odd,* he thought. *It's heavier than I expected.* One of the rollers squeaked when he pulled the swivel chair closer to the oak rolltop desk in his courthouse office. Purdy had left a stack of papers to be read, signed, sent out to who knew where, or filed. A list of prisoners held in the county jail was dated several months past. He'd have to look at fixing that. There were notes about upcoming court cases. What was he supposed to do about those? There was a lot to learn, being a sheriff.

"Beg pardon, Sheriff."

Tilman turned to find a well-dressed man standing in the open doorway to his office. He'd have to rearrange the room. He didn't like to be surprised by visitors. He stood and offered his hand. "Tilman Wagner," he said. "And you are . . . ?"

"Prosper Charbonneau. May we talk?"

"I thought you carried a different name, Charbonneau."

"I was known as 'Smiley' long ago, but I have changed my ways." Charbonneau paused and, with a tight smile, looked at Tilman. "I believe you also carry a past. . . ."

Tilman nodded in acknowledgment. "Point taken. Come in and have a seat."

"If I may," Charbonneau said, closing the door, "I'd like to speak in private." Charbonneau pulled a chair so that his back was not to the door, then settled himself. After a moment his eyes met Tilman's, all pretense of the earlier refined manners gone. "Purdy's sudden death was unfortunate."

"I understand you paid all expenses to have the body shipped

17

back to Tennessee for burial," Tilman said. "Were you and Purdy friends?"

"Not exactly friends. We had business connections."

"County business?"

"Not exactly," Charbonneau answered. "But as sheriff, he was in a position to help me, and of course I made sure that he was compensated for his troubles both in cash and in advantages. I in turn gave him information of value in his law-enforcement duties."

Tilman nodded, wondering why the man was being so careful with his words.

"That's why I'm here. Just because he's dead, I see no reason things have to change. You and I are men who understand the ways of the world. Power brings riches, and riches bring more power. As sheriff, you're well placed in the county to know what goes on, who is doing what, and because of that your influence can send one man into poverty and another to fabulous wealth. Life can be enjoyable for those who are alert for opportunity."

"How do I fit in?" Tilman asked, although he thought he already had an idea.

"In your work, are you a man to hold to the letter of the law? Or are you one who is more inclined to deem the larger spirit of the law more important?"

"I don't believe I follow you."

"Are you one who can arrange an understanding—by that I mean, can you overlook certain small transgressions if no one is hurt?"

Tilman listened, his face revealing nothing. He controlled his rising interest. If this was what he thought it was . . . Tilman steadied himself, then cleared his throat. "I'd like to know more, Mr. Charbonneau. I'll admit that in the past I've stood on both sides of the fence. I was younger then and did what I had to do to get what I wanted."

Charbonneau nodded but said nothing.

"Let me get this straight," Tilman said. "This 'understanding' you're talking about. You mean to say that Oliver Purdy turned a blind eye to certain things as long as nobody really got hurt and everybody was happy. And you want me to go along the way he did. Well, what are those 'certain things'?"

"We can talk more," Charbonneau answered, "when there is need. We all have our ways of doing things, ways we are accustomed to, and we hope to continue those ways. Purdy's unfortunate death need not interrupt things. I simply ask if you're willing to work with me in a mutually beneficial relationship."

"I get your drift." Tilman paused, looking directly at Charbonneau. "If I say no deal?"

"Then I would be disappointed and would work against you in the coming election. You and I will part ways, and I never came to see you today."

"One more thing. Your daughter is married to Jim Peel up in Granite."

"Marie Fleur, yes."

"My wife tells me she is both lovely and educated," Tilman continued. "I haven't met her or her husband, I'm afraid."

"She is the picture of her late mother, and she studied at L'Academie des jeune filles—that is, The Academy for Young Ladies—in New Orleans."

"What does she know of your past?" Tilman asked.

"Very little, and I hope to keep it that way," Charbonneau answered. "She has no need to know of such matters."

"Was Peel sheriff before or after they got married?"

"Before."

"I see. Give me a few days to think it over, and we'll talk some more."

When Tilman had closed the door after Charbonneau, he stood before a window and looked across the Arkansas River to the rising mass of Free Gold Hill. His hands clenched into fists. It hadn't taken long for that Charbonneau fellow to make himself known. He took a deep breath. A smooth dealer, that one. Too smooth.

Tilman knew he'd have to be careful. Catherine had told him that Sheriff Purdy had been on this man's payroll. And she was right. Had it been that obvious? How had he not known? Could it be possible that Prosper had had his daughter marry Jim Peel so he could have an inside man in the county government? What kind of man would do that? Tilman had seen Mrs. Peel from a distance and knew her to be a beautiful young woman. Remembering the "Smiley" of the old days, he could only wonder why Charbonneau had brought her back here to the Valley.

Those carefully chosen words Charbonneau had spoken so easily raised warning signals in Tilman's mind, which was now racing. *What's going on here? What kind of business is this fellow involved in? How much money is changing hands here? Who's involved and why? What does he ask in return— that I sell my soul? It seems Purdy did so. I'm going to have to talk this over with Butter. He has a way of getting down to the meat of things.*

Chapter Five

Several days earlier, during a welcome-home dinner at Butter Pegram's ranch near the town of Nathrop a few miles south of Buena Vista, Tilman had explained to Butter how he'd come to be the new sheriff of Chaffee County. But he had not mentioned any of his concerns about the recent spate of robberies around the county. At the end of the day, when Tilman and his family loaded up a buckboard to head home, Tilman had asked Butter to come by for a talk. Now the two old friends savored hot cups of thick black coffee in the sheriff's office in the county courthouse, and talk flowed easily.

"Don't worry about Neala," Butter assured Tilman. "She's got her hands full settling into the house and keeping up with the young'uns."

"Who's going to be running your ranch?"

"Uncle Seef—my daddy's little brother, Josephus. He hired a couple of fellers to dig some irrigation ditches for me, and, long as he's there, he agreed to act as my foreman for sixty dollars a month and food."

"Mighty convenient," Tilman said.

"Well, he ain't much of a cook on his own, and he hates batchin' it, so he'll do. Me an' you've been down some rough trails, and I ain't so sure about what you've got yourself into with this sheriff job. I reckon you'll be needing my help." Butter refilled his mug. The man never seemed to get his fill of coffee.

"I appreciate your sidin' me again, *Deputy* Pegram."

"Badge and bullets?"

"Sure. Bring your own horse and tack, and the county will pay feed and livery costs."

"Knowed there was a catch," Butter said. "Now, what haven't you told me?"

From a drawer Tilman pulled recent issues of the Buena Vista and Leadville newspapers. "Take a look at these, and you'll get some of it. Papers are screaming about 'gangs of highwaymen' and 'stickup men' behind every tree and rock. You'd think somebody's getting robbed right here in town every day!" He pulled one of the papers from the stack and pointed to the headlines. "There's a story about poor old Oliver Purdy, the sheriff before me."

"What else?" Butter asked. "This can't be all of it, or I wouldn't be here."

"I had company as soon as I got in here." Tilman watched for Butter's reaction. " 'Smiley' Charbonneau. Goes by Prosper Charbonneau now, all dressed to the nines and trying to look real dignified. Until he opened his mouth, that is."

Butter had listened carefully, his full attention on Tilman. "Why," he said, "I remember 'Smiley' Charbonneau. When you first came looking for Dan's killer, Bill Ward owned half of this town, and Smiley owned the other. And I don't know who was worse."

"Well, it seems Prosper and Purdy did a little side business, with Purdy getting his palms greased for looking the other way. Must have been real profitable, and Charbonneau pretty much, in a roundabout way, offered me the same deal."

"My, oh, my. That wasn't the smartest move. Wish I could have heard that."

"I told him I needed a day or two to think, but I'm sure he knows I'm not interested."

"He'll bear watching, then, I think." Butter looked at Tilman. "Tilman, if he's used to getting around the law, then he'll want you to be gone quickly if you stand in his way."

"I know. That's one of the reasons I'm glad you're here to help."

The two men spent the day discussing the recent holdups and bank robbery and trying to come to a starting place for finding the robbers. Butter, ever the good listener, asked a few questions to clarify a point or to expand on something Tilman said.

"That's a lot to take in," Butter observed. "Let me think on it some. For now, what's your plan?"

"Same as usual," Tilman admitted.

"Hah!" Butter laughed. "You ain't got one! I was afraid of that."

"Well, it worked when we went after Bill Ward here in town, and it worked down at Fort Davis."

"Where I got shot," Butter said, waving the stub of his right index finger at Tilman.

"Worked in New Mexico too."

"They say God looks after fools and little children," Butter said, "and you sure ain't no kid!"

Chapter Six

Six months earlier

This is the last time!" Prosper Charbonneau paced the room in anger. "I am not going to cover any more of your losses. I promised your mother when you arrived here last year that you would quit the gambling."

Marcel Devereaux, Prosper's only nephew, stood quietly before him. "Yes, Uncle. That was our agreement."

"Today a man delivered these markers signed by you." Prosper threw a handful of papers into Marcel's face, and they scattered to the floor. "If you want to work for me, the gambling must cease."

Marcel, in looks a younger, thinner version of Prosper, was unmoved by his uncle's outburst.

"Do you have any idea how much you owe to the Looking Glass Saloon in Leadville? And that is only one of the places you frequent."

"Uncle . . ." Marcel stopped before he began. He knew his uncle wasn't buying any of his excuses. With arms slightly raised and his palms outward, he shrugged.

The gesture was not lost on Prosper, who made much the same gesture when trying to convince someone of his sincerity. How like a son was his nephew! "Marcel, these are no idle threats. The man who left these told me you have a week to pay, and they want it all. No more time or partial payments." Prosper moved behind his desk, his anger under control, to prepare a cigar, one of his Cuban imports, and lit it. From a

24

bottom drawer of his desk he withdrew a cash box and opened it. "I am going to give you this because I want this debt paid and you out of trouble, but, Marcel"—Prosper placed the cigar on a crystal smoker—"listen carefully. I am not doing this again. The next time, they can have you." He quietly counted out the amount Marcel owed. "Take this, and pay off the debt. Then come back here. I have a job for you that will even us out."

Marcel accepted the money. He started to offer his thanks, but he knew his uncle wanted none. The more he learned about his Uncle Prosper, the more he came to understand that he was dangerous, a man not to be crossed. As a man would not provoke a Louisiana bayou cottonmouth moccasin, so was his uncle not to be regarded lightly. Marcel would have to take care not to step from the frying pan into the fire. Prosper was where he was, not due to gracious deeds, but because he was ruthless and clever. Marcel would watch and learn. One day this would all be his, *if* he could keep his uncle from throwing him out or, worse still, killing him in anger.

Prosper reached behind his desk to lift a large basket tied with lavender bows and holly. He handed the basket to Marcel.

"On the way back from Leadville, turn aside in Granite to visit that lovely daughter of mine. Marie Fleur misses New Orleans coffee and fine teas, so I have put together this gift package for her. Now get out of here."

"Yes, Uncle. I'll be happy to see her."

After Marcel left the room, Prosper thoughtfully took up his cigar. He knew the Leadville men to be merciless. Once, he had been like them. No, not simply *like* them, for in truth he was one of the worst of them. But, one by one, his kind had been shot down in the dead of night, or run out of town, or caught, tried, and condemned to rot in the penitentiary. He had come to see that the old, wide-open, rough-and-tumble boom-town days were in the past. He wanted to live, and to do so he had to adapt to progress, at least outwardly. He'd made up his mind that he'd be a state senator one day or even a U.S. Congressman. He didn't care which. He wanted power and riches, and he'd do whatever it took to achieve them. Controlling the county in so many ways and having a good hold on the neighboring communities had taken him years of work. After Bill Ward, his main competitor in town, was killed, he'd understood that he must change his ways or die. When Mahonville was renamed Buena Vista, he had set out to clean up his image and rebuild himself. He'd even donated the bell to the new community church, while he attended St. Rose de Lima Catholic Church. His mother had taught him well.

But what was Marcel going to do? In many ways his own nephew was a stranger to him. Prosper intended for Marcel to take over when he moved on to the capitol, but he needed a person he could trust to help. Prosper's business affairs with saloons and girls and such appeared beyond reproach from the outside, for his ties were carefully layered and distanced. Still, he couldn't resist taking a more active hand in occasional disreputable but profitable deals—after all, a man thrived on danger—to build his political war chest, support his lifestyle, and especially to finance the new mansion.

Chapter Seven

Marie Fleur Peel née Charbonneau sat framed in a wide window bordered with colorful stained-glass insets that her father had bought for her. Prosper's only child had inherited his ebony hair, Creole coloring, and her dead mother's figure. Marie Fleur displayed the perfect hourglass shape, including the kind of tiny waist that some women starved themselves for days in order to have. Marie Fleur loved to eat and drink and knew that she intrigued men, but it didn't really matter. Like her father, she had a sense of longing for the unattainable, but, unlike him, she had no idea what that might be. She had hoped her marriage would bring her peace. Jim Peel loved her, but they seemed to speak two different languages. She had hoped that having children would help, but after three miscarriages, the doctor had told her there would be no young ones in her life. So she waited. She didn't know for what, but she waited.

The window had been a housewarming gift for her new house in Granite when she and Jim had married. Originally part of a decaying cathedral outside Paris, the window was brought to America by a merchant ship's captain for his home in New Orleans, but the captain had died before construction was completed. Charbonneau's cotton factor from his early days on the docks had found it for him and had it shipped to Colorado Springs and on to Granite by train.

At the Granite station it had taken four laid-off miners to lift it onto a flatbed mule-drawn wagon and haul it to the Peel home. Charbonneau had hired carpenters from Leadville to come down and install it in the west-facing cupola to capture the view of great looming mountains behind the town. The house itself was Victorian with twists and curls and fancy accents, painted deep red with white trim. Marie Fleur often saw passersby admiring the lovely two-story home set above the east bank of the river.

Standing at her window, she smiled at the irony of the whole thing. She had expected to be the wife of the sheriff of Chaffee County. Her father had had a dream that she would be well connected with the important people in this mineral-rich district of Colorado. The mines were producing steadily, and the times were glorious, and Sheriff Jim Peel became a man of influence in his own right. But then the county seat had gone to Buena Vista, and her husband lost his bid for reelection. Granite's mines went bust, and the hydraulic and placer mining companies moved out after hosing away most of the riverbanks north of town, leaving a confusion of huge piles of rocks, rubble, and rusting water pipes. Men simply walked away from their shanties and dugouts. Courts adjourned, and workers boarded up the courthouse. Prices on town lots plummeted. Granite was close to becoming a ghost town. That was that.

A gusty north wind buffeted the house, abated, and blustered once again. The *tick-tock* of the mantel clock echoed from the other room, the only sound intruding on the oppressive silence of her empty house. Marie Fleur's shoulders slumped.

"Hello, *ma chérie*."

Marie Fleur turned in surprise, her stylish bustle getting in the way as usual, brushing against an empty teacup she had placed on a side table. It shattered on the polished wood floor. Her mouth turned down in bitterness. In the doorway stood a rakishly handsome young man, his jet-black hair pomaded and slicked back. He sported a pencil mustache across his upper lip that angled sharply upward under his nose, marking him as a man who kept up with styles currently all the rage among the sporting set back in Baton Rouge.

"Marcel, I wasn't expecting company."

"So I see. Why the frown?"

"I broke the cup. One more thing gone wrong."

Marcel held out his arms, smiling.

Marie Fleur crossed the room to kiss her cousin on both cheeks, European style, and tugged him along to sit by her on a burgundy velvet settee. "How did you escape from Papa? Why are you in Granite, Marcel? Never mind. Thank God you're here. I think I am going crazy."

His cousin's apparent loneliness surprised Marcel. *So many questions!* "Um, where is Jim?" Marcel looked appreciatively around at the stylish clutter of costly furniture, pictures, thick Turkish rugs, and knickknacks Prosper had lavished on his daughter until the room could not possibly hold anything else. A small hand-carved cradle now covered by a large knitted shawl was placed to catch the sun's warmth. He thought, *What is this? Almost but not quite out of sight, out of mind.*

"He is probably out beating up drunks and out-of-work miners." Marie Fleur pouted. "He hasn't been the same since Oliver Purdy was elected sheriff. You know that was supposed to be Jim's job, don't you? Papa promised." Marie Fleur arose, shaking her coal black hair—the same color as her cousin's—so hard that the ringlets shook and one slipped from its clasp to brush her delicate neck. "I don't understand."

"It's really quite simple, cousin. Purdy was one of the favored, a local boy backed by the county commissioners, also local boys. It is as always in most places." Marcel came to stand by Marie Fleur, looking out the window as the wind set an aspen limb raking against one corner of the house. Evening shadows were starting to lengthen across the dirt street. A desolate scene of emptiness and the great expanse of blue sky above the stark mountains lay before them. The cousins stood framed by the window, she disillusioned and unhappy, he shrewdly biding his time. "How do you stand the constant wind here, *chérie?* I think I would lose my mind."

"Don't 'dear' me, cousin. I'm no French Quarter tart hungry for your flattery. Why are you here? I've never known you to be concerned about my health."

"Do you remember when we were children? How we used to hide in my tree house to plan our lives when we grew up? How we were going to have lives filled with intrigue and adventure? How no one was going to tell us how to live our lives?"

"I wanted to be a privateer, a female Jean Lafitte, the scourge of the high seas!" The memory of a simpler time took away the darkness of her mood. "And all you wanted was to become the most cunning and successful riverboat gambler on the Mississippi."

Marcel knuckled his mustache. "I still want to be that."

"What do you really want, Marcel?" Marie Fleur motioned for him to follow her into the dining room.

"A drink. First I really want a drink."

She opened the aspen liquor cabinet that Jim had made before they married and removed a bottle. "Would you like a pastis?"

"Of course."

Half filling two glasses with the clear liqueur, she added water from a small pitcher. The liquid turned milky, and the scent of licorice filled the room.

As she handed a glass to Marcel, she glanced furtively over his shoulder.

"Who are you looking for? Your father? Jim?" Marcel drained his glass and reached past Marie Fleur to refill it. "That is what I'm wondering about."

"But I'm not looking for anyone. I . . ." She stopped in midsentence. "Oh, never mind." She sat on one of the high-backed chairs, the strong drink loosening her inhibitions. "I thought when I married, I'd have children. I thought I'd have the life Papa promised me if I did what he wanted. He sent me away to a convent to keep me from knowing what he did, but I heard talk. The sisters didn't always know we heard, and they loved to gossip. Papa was somehow connected with the bars and gambling and places men frequent." She stopped. "To be honest, I know he thought he was doing his best for me, but"—she paused—"I am too much like my papa. There is a fire that burns inside me to push against the boundaries others set for me. I want to live and enjoy my life."

"Your father treats me like I am the help, not his only nephew." Marcel crossed the room to the cabinet, his small feet shod in plain but comfortable black shoes that belied his taste for all things expensive. He turned to face Marie Fleur.

"Uncle told me you have learned to ride and shoot. Is that how you enjoy life?"

"What else is there to do here? Jim is a good man but fifteen years older than I and very staid. He is an excellent shot and horseman, and so I asked him to help me learn these things." She laughed bitterly, a faraway look in her eyes. "I told him I needed protection when he was away. But there is no protection from the madness of day after day of nothing but the wind and snow and vast openness here. I want lights and music and fun!" A hard gust of wind shook the house and, like fingers probing for an opening, set up a breathy moaning around the eaves. She drew herself up, as if returning from somewhere else. "Hear the wind? That's what I mean. Well, where is this conversation going?" She smiled. "Have you been gambling again? You know what Papa said."

"Of course I have, *dear*. I just got unlucky a few times up in Leadville. My uncle thinks I am giving it up, and I want to keep him thinking that way." He looked carefully at Marie Fleur. "How would you like to go adventuring with me, 'Mademoiselle Lafitte'? It would give you something to fill your dreary days, and no harm would come to anyone. You might be a little less bored with your life."

After a moment of hesitation she looked over the rim of her glass. "Tell me all, cousin." She smiled. "Tell me all."

Chapter Eight

Present day

Jim? Where did you go? Cook is ready for us. . . ." Marie
Fleur stopped. Her husband stood with a whiskey glass in one
hand, gazing out the cupola window as the autumn sun sank
behind the mountains. "Penny for your thoughts?" Marie Fleur
gently took the glass as she turned for the kitchen. Watching
Jim, she stumbled over the cradle, the drink sloshing onto her
hand. Her anger flared. "I don't know why I don't get rid of this
thing. It just gets in the way."

"It's okay, Fleur. It really isn't that important. You and I
will manage without little Peels." A strong arm drew her close
as her husband led her into the dining room. For the moment
Marie Fleur had the husband she had envisioned back, and all
seemed right. But she knew better.

They sat down to their meal. "I must say, I'm glad you got
Mai Lee to come do the laundry and cooking, though." Jim,
with napkin tucked into his shirt collar, smiled as he filled his
plate. Marie Fleur insisted on red wine with her meal, so Peel
filled their glasses. He'd have preferred a beer. He got a mind
picture of himself in a saloon saying, "*Barkeep, another* vin
rouge." What a fight that would start! He smiled at the thought.

"For a Chinaman, he's a pretty good cook. Hard to understand, though."

"Papa offered to bring up a cook from New Orleans for us."

"Not now, Fleur, not again. Let it go."

They ate quietly while, outside, the late-fall chill of the

Colorado high country cloaked the house. Marie Fleur listened to the silence creeping through the house. The sadness came. Once more she asked herself how such a promising future could turn so quickly to distantly formal pretense and existence. Hers was a world of small talk and words that had no meaning. Once again she looked at Jim and wondered how such a strong man could have gotten involved with her father. What if, she wondered, what if she had never consented to be his wife? He needed a woman to support him and lift him up, and she definitely failed at being that woman.

"Marie?" Jim reached out to touch the left hand she'd clenched into a small hard fist beside her plate. "Are you daydreaming? I asked if you'd seen Marcel lately." Jim refilled her wineglass. "I heard he was gambling again at the Silver King Saloon in Leadville last weekend."

"Surely not, Jim. Papa said he'd make Marcel wish he'd never worked for him if he got into trouble again." Fleur knew with certainty that Marcel was tempting fate. She had better warn him that people were talking and that such talk would surely reach her father's ears sooner rather than later.

She placed her napkin on the table. The meal was over. Jim left her with the dishes. She knew that by the time she finished, he'd be in his big chair by the fire, sound asleep, and would remain there throughout the night. Since she'd lost the last baby, he'd slept in that chair. Sometimes he slept at the office under the pretense that he was needed there, but she knew better. He feared for her life with another pregnancy. Maybe, she mused, he was stronger than she thought. The night wind roared down from the mountain slopes to push against the sides of the house. The roof creaked. She shuddered and tried to remember better days.

Chapter Nine

The pealing of the church bell signaled to all of Buena Vista that the celebration was starting.

"What a joyful noise! I can hardly hear the babies," Catherine said as she and Neala made their way from the church's new nursery room, where the twins and Neala's two smallest children were safely playing during the family social. Prosper Charbonneau had donated the church bell, and one of the mining companies had donated money for a steeple.

Neala covered her ears. "Well, it certainly is loud." Nearby, Neala's oldest son played tag with his next younger brother.

The two women surveyed the bustling crowd filling the fellowship hall. Many of the families new to the community were present as well as some of the older and more prominent ones. Some came to be part of the church, while many others came for the food. Church socials were known for plenty of biscuits, loaves of country bread, fried chicken, hams, venison and elk, turkey, and both canned and fresh vegetables. Of course, then there were desserts.

Neala leaned close to Catherine. "Have you heard about the plans Mr. Charbonneau has for a new house?"

"Yes, I have. They say he's building on the road toward Granite."

"Mr. Pegram"—Neala habitually referred to her husband, Butter, in that formal way—"Mr. Pegram said that Mr. Charbonneau is trying to copy the Robinson home in Cañon City."

"Yes, but I heard he wants one even bigger and better."

"There's who we should ask, I think." Catherine nodded her head for Neala to look across to the far side of the room, where a lovely young woman sat by herself. "She'll know."

"Is that Charbonneau's daughter?" Neala studied the young woman before turning back to Catherine. "How do you come to know her?" Neala blushed. "I mean, Mr. Pegram told me about the old days, when that Charbonneau was not the kind of man any decent woman would admit to knowing."

"When he first came here, he didn't bring her, because her mother had died—they say the yellow fever took her. He sent the girl off to school and waited until she was grown. By then he was starting to make himself respectable. I never made her acquaintance until she finished school in New Orleans and came to live with her father. First thing he did was set about marrying her off to Jim Peel. I think he planned for Jim to be the new county sheriff." Catherine hooked her arm in Neala's. "But it seems the people of Buena Vista like to stick to their known little world, so they elected Oliver Purdy, God rest his soul, instead of Jim."

"Mr. Pegram says her father is a man of ambition." Neala nodded. "He's a big fish, I reckon—too big for this little puddle of a town." Neala squeezed Catherine's hand. "I suppose since Tilman is married to you and lives here, he's known, and they trusted him with the job."

The two women made their way through a steady murmur of people eating and laughing. A pleasant, homey atmosphere filled the space like the sweet fragrance of spring flowers filling the warm air above a meadow.

After greeting the younger woman, Catherine made the introductions. Catherine said to Neala, "Marie Fleur lives in Granite with her husband, the town marshal, and she is Mr. Charbonneau's only child. She visits Buena Vista often."

"I remember the first time I met Catherine," Marie Fleur said to Neala. "She was one of the few women gracious enough to acknowledge me when I arrived from New Orleans. My father was not always known for his good deeds, and most of the town 'ladies' chose to exclude me socially. But Catherine has been kind, so I will always be grateful for that."

"Where is James, Catherine?" Marie Fleur looked around the room. "He must be nearly grown."

"James is running the ranch these days while his father is filling in as sheriff, and, yes, he stands about a foot taller than me. But you, Marie Fleur, what have you been doing?"

Marie Fleur adjusted her seat so that she didn't crush the bustle of her soft blue velvet dress. "I stay busy up in the windy town of Granite." She laughed softly, her cheeks rosy from the cool fall air. "We seem always to be attending some function or another in Leadville, or Papa needs me to come and do something for him." She looked around, and Catherine sensed that Marie Fleur had other things on her mind.

Neala was aware of the younger woman's preoccupation as well. "We don't mean to pry."

"Oh, no, you're not. I'm sorry." Marie Fleur turned to Neala. "Are you a newcomer to Colorado, Mrs. Pegram?"

"Mr. Pegram and I recently came from Texas. We met when he and Mr. Wagner came there several years ago. We married, and three little stair-step boys and one girl came along, so I don't often get out to visit."

When the talk turned to children, Catherine suddenly remembered that Marie Fleur had recently lost a baby and had had no luck having any others. "I'm sorry, Marie Fleur. I . . ."

"Catherine, I'm fine. I know I'm not meant to be a mother." Marie Fleur laughed nervously and changed the subject. "So, what would I know about? I heard you talking as you came over to sit."

"Oh, that. Well, Neala asked about your father's new house, and I said you'd be the authority on that."

"Well, all I know is that my papa has always been a dreamer. He wants a home larger than the mansion in Cañon City. Do you know the one I mean? That one near the river that has three floors, five bedrooms, offices, studies, parlors, a gazebo, and a carriage house with quarters for the maids and grooms. I think he has gone over his head this time." Marie Fleur leaned closer to the older women and lowered her voice as if to share a secret. "I think it is too much, and I tell him so, but he pays me no mind. I don't know who is going to live in such a house. He envisions small children to carry on, and I know of none. Maybe if my cousin Marcel marries, that will change things, but"—Marie shrugged in helpless resignation—"I do not see Marcel ever settling down and becoming a father."

"Do I hear my name being taken in vain?" Marcel appeared behind his cousin as if by magic. Marcel was the very *beau idéal* of Boston or New York City. A fancy silk vest set off the tailored gray wool suit carefully accented by a bright red handkerchief in his coat pocket. His handmade shoes were expensive leather and very small, almost dainty.

"*Excusez moi*"—Marcel half bowed to Catherine—"but I need to borrow Marie Fleur for a moment, *s'il vous plaît*." Marcel always played the charmer with an attractive woman, married or not. Most women responded, but this one was suddenly cool, unapproachable.

"Catherine, Neala, I have enjoyed your company." Marie Fleur rose, and she and Marcel went out the side door of the fellowship hall.

Neala elbowed Catherine. "He's a handsome devil with a fine accent, but I don't trust him for some reason. He's too smooth for my tastes. And such *feet!*"

Catherine looked puzzled. "What about his feet?"

"They're little bitty things!" Neala lifted her skirt hem to reveal sturdy leather boots. "I don't think I could get one of his shoes over my big toe, let alone wear it." The two women shared a laugh at such a ridiculous thought.

"Well, I'm inclined to agree with you. He came to help his uncle—oh, it was several months ago—and he seems always to be in a hurry. Tilman says Charbonneau is a hard taskmaster, so maybe he's a different man than we think."

"Beg pardon. Have you ladies seen my wife?" Jim Peel crossed the room with Tilman and Butter to stand before Catherine and Neala. "I thought I saw her come this way."

"She and Marcel have only just left us." Catherine stood, entwining her arm in Tilman's. "Have you eaten yet, Mr. Wagner?"

"No, ma'am, not yet. I'm famished. Jim? Care to join us?"

"You all go on. I'll go look for Marie Fleur."

Chapter Ten

Nobody paid any attention when Marcel and Marie Fleur left the church. The cousins casually strolled a short distance to Prosper's downtown office above the First Carbonate National Bank. Once inside, they quickly changed from their elegant town clothes into rough workmen's garb, Marie Fleur laughing girlishly behind the dressing screen.

"Hurry!" Marcel urged.

Soon they rode side by side south of town, their horses at a fast trot. Marcel pointed to the lone rider coming into view a short distance ahead. "There he is. He just forded the river."

Marie Fleur, wearing britches and sitting astride her mount, raised a gloved hand and tugged up her bandanna so that only her eyes were visible below the wide-brimmed hat she wore. "Cover, Marcel, for we don't want him to recognize you." They drew closer to the other rider, long dusters covering their rough work clothes and boots.

"Are you absolutely sure he has the money?" she asked,

"I'm sure, *chérie*. I prepared the express pouch myself."

Marie Fleur reached out with her quirt and swatted her cousin's shoulder. "What do you mean? You said this money came from Dutch Annie's cribs in the alley behind the hotel."

"And so it does."

Marie Fleur hesitated, unsure of what she'd heard. Normally a self-controlled woman not easily ruffled, she was at a loss for words. Already excited by what she was about to do, she felt her emotions flicker and then flame out. The world fell out from under her, a feeling of hugely disappointed realization. Marie Fleur sagged, feeling older than her years. "But Papa told me he was finished with that business and that he no longer owned any of those women."

Perhaps every daughter finally saw her father, not as a knight in shining armor, but as the kind of man he really was. But for Marie Fleur, it couldn't have come at a worse time.

"He lied, didn't he?" She fairly shouted the angry words. "He has never stopped doing all the things he tried to hide by sending me away. He believes that I so trust, I am so sheltered, that I would never learn how he survives. My father, a panderer! Those things the sisters whispered about—the knifings, the beatings. They're true, aren't they?"

"I think, *chérie,* that now is not the time. We have work to do. We can talk later. Am I not right?"

"Don't call me *dear!*" Marie Fleur's anger subsided into icy wrath. "I am my father's daughter. I slipped away from church and my husband to become a highway robber, and my papa doesn't know!"

Anyone who saw her now would see nothing more than a slightly built but agitated young man who let his gun do the talking—that was how she'd be described.

Her hand caressed the small revolver holstered under the duster, and she spurred her mount into a hard, ground-eating gallop. "Let's go, Marcel."

An unsuspecting Hube Kirk let the mule pick his own pace, an easygoing walk. Laid off from his job at a placer mine below Twin Lakes, he would soon be going back home to a hardscrabble farm outside Jackson, Tennessee. He'd rushed to Colorado to follow a dream of gold nuggets by the dozens begging to be picked up in every streambed, but instead of finding riches, he'd ruined his health working to make somebody else wealthy.

A nagging cough worried him, but he'd not mentioned that in the letters home he paid a fellow to write for him. He'd never gotten around to learning to read and write more than his own name. His hands were swollen twice-normal size all the time, and his fingers had lost their flexibility from nearly constant immersion in icy waters. He couldn't stand the cold anymore. With his poke almost empty, the delivery job couldn't have come at a better time. They even gave him the mule—his to keep—and a pistol. He could keep that too.

"Take the express bag to Salida," old Charbonneau had told him. "Go to the Elkhorn Saloon across from the Railroad Hospital. Ask for Mr. Jones."

Hube was jolted from his reverie when two riders hauled up alongside his old mule, their horses lathered and dancing. Then he saw the gun.

One of the riders motioned with that gun. "Get 'em up."

Hube got 'em up. "Don't shoot me, mister."

Marie Fleur urged her horse closer, lifted the pistol from Hube's holster, and tossed it aside.

"We won't." Marcel said. "All we want is that express pouch, so hand it over."

"I ain't got the key." Hube released the ties, and Marie Fleur took the pouch from him. She took a small yellow flower from her own shirt and stuffed it into the pocket of Hube's shirt. Her gloves covered her hands, but Hube was shaking so hard, he had his eyes closed in fear anyway.

Marcel laughed. "We won't need a key!"

"Are you gonna let me go?" Hube slowly opened an eye and looked at the robbers.

"Ride on, and you'd better not stop before you get to Smeltertown, or else we'll come an' get you."

Marie Fleur lashed Hube's mule with her quirt and shouted, "Hyah! Hyah!"

The animal lurched into a stiff-legged trot, and Hube nearly lost his seat.

She pulled the bandanna from her face. Flashing an exuberant grin, Marie Fleur drew her pistol and fired several shots into the air. The mule trotted even faster, Hube rocking in the saddle, both swollen mitts grasping the saddle horn. His battered old hat rolled into the dusty road behind him.

Thirty minutes later Marie Fleur was back in the church hall, checking to make sure her dress and shoes were correct as she patted her hair. Seeing Jim standing by the picnic table, she slipped up beside him and took his arm. "My goodness,

Jim. Where have you been? I was afraid you'd left me. Marcel and I went looking for you. We split up, but finally I found you."

"I wondered where you'd gotten off to, Marie. I was busy talking with folks and lost track of the time." Jim guided her to a stack of plates. "Let's eat before they start packing things up. I think the choir program begins in the new building in a few minutes."

Marcel made his way unnoticed into the building in time to hear the choir sing.

Chapter Eleven

Tilman sat alone at a table in the Roundhouse Saloon across the street from the town's railroad station. His back was to a corner with a double window offering a good view of the street. Only a few customers sat at nearby tables, while several others leaned on the bar. Outside, a man paused on the plank sidewalk to peer through the front window. Seeing Tilman, he turned and came through the front door, heading straight for Tilman's table.

"U.S. Deputy Marshal Tom Early, from Denver," the man announced in a booming voice. "Mind if I join you?"

Men at the other tables turned to look. Even the bartender glanced up from polishing glasses to see who spoke with such authority. At Tilman's openhanded gesture, Early pulled out a chair and sat. Pulling his chair closer to Tilman, he wasted no time.

"You're Wagner, the new sheriff?"

"I am. What can I do for you?"

"You know about the miners' strike at some of the Leadville mines?" Early asked. "There was a killin' done. Somebody shot a Federal mine inspector."

"It's been in the newspapers."

"The U.S. Marshal in Denver sent me to get the man who done it," Early said, "an Irishman named Mulrooney and his pard. I hear they're laying low here in Buena Vista."

Conversation at nearby tables ceased as men eavesdropped on the lawmen. A U.S. Deputy Marshal coming to town was a big thing. Whatever they heard would be discussed and embellished at other bars and be all over the town before the day ended.

"I'm just a county sheriff, new on the job, so I have to ask about your jurisdiction."

"The judge—Stevens—he said we have jurisdiction. It says right here"—Tom Early pulled a sheaf of folded papers from the inside pocket of his coat—"that U.S. Deputy Marshals for the Federal District Court of Colorado may make arrests for murder, manslaughter, assault with intent to kill or to maim, attempts to murder, and so forth and so on, with or without a warrant." The papers went unopened back into his pocket.

"I want that man Mulrooney and a fellow they call 'The Tamper,' his pard." Early continued, "Killing of a government man has been done, foul murder, a woman made a widow, and her two children made fatherless. I'm here to arrest the killers and haul 'em back to Denver to be hanged. I wanted you to know I'll be around your town for a day or so."

"I appreciate your coming to see me." Tilman eyed the deputy marshal. "I assume there'll be a trial in there somewhere?"

"Oh, they'll go before Judge Stevens all right," Early said, reaching up to scratch at his two-day beard stubble. "And if the judge can keep some slick lawyer from selling a bill of goods to the jury, then there'll be two hangings," he muttered behind his hand.

Tilman studied the deputy. Tom Early combed his thin hair across a prematurely balding pate. He guessed the marshal's worn dark suit and collarless boiled shirt with frayed cuffs was probably the only suit he owned. The man's whiskey-deep voice and the smell of tobacco smoke that surrounded him spoke of a rough life. As Tilman watched, Early shifted uncomfortably in his chair, then raised his right ankle to rest on his left knee. The man's boot soles were muddy, but then, Buena Vista's streets were no more than dirt, gravel, and mud. Paper showed through a hole worn in the sole of his boot.

To break the silence, Early explained, "A deputy marshal gets paid at the rate of six cents a mile traveled, and two dollars per arrest or served process, so coming all the way from

Denver and managing two arrests might earn me a profit. Of course, it ain't all gravy. The U.S. Marshal gets a quarter of that."

"I've heard no mention of a Mulrooney around town," Tilman said, "but names don't mean much."

"I have some wanted posters in my hotel room," Early said. "I'll bring 'em to your office." Early stood, nodded to the bartender, and disappeared through the door as fast as he'd arrived.

The customers at the nearest table, deep in discussion about the two wanted men, didn't even notice when Tilman left a few minutes later.

Chapter Twelve

Tilman had hardly gotten back to his desk when Early loomed in his doorway. Tilman couldn't help but see that the man was empty-handed. "Did you find Mulrooney already?" Tilman asked, looking as perplexed as he felt. What was he missing?

Early helped himself to a cup of coffee, dragged a chair to Tilman's desk, and sat. "Before I left Leadville, I got a telegram from Sheriff Dick Hyde over in Fairplay. Mulrooney and his pard are cooling their heels in the Park County Jail." He rolled an unlit stick match in the corner of his mouth. "I'll collect them in a day or so. They ain't going nowhere. That Hyde's gettin' a little long in the tooth, but he can still take care of those two with one hand behind his back."

"So what you said earlier was a dodge."

"Well, sure." He grinned. "I needed to talk to you and didn't want anybody to suspect why I'm really here."

"Go ahead. I'm listening." Tilman got coffee for himself. "This have anything to do with the problems we've been having around these parts?"

"Somebody around here's been lifting gold and silver," Early said.

Tilman leaned back in his chair, looked out the window, and snorted, "Humph. You don't say."

"Hold on. I don't mean the penny-ante high grading stuff at the mines," Early said. "I'm talking about some real money here. When ore from the mines here in the Valley gets milled, the gold and silver alloy is molded into bullion bars. After they cool, the solid bars get shipped to the U.S. Mint in Denver."

45

"That's a regular sight here in town," Tilman said, wondering where Early was going with this. "They go out by train." He stood and stretched. For a man used to working outdoors, it was hard sitting inside. Being behind a desk got tiresome real quick. It wasn't that he looked for trouble, but a little fracas or a fistfight might liven things up a bit. Early studied him, evidently not sure the sheriff was listening to him.

"I'm sorry," Tilman said. "So they ship the bars. And then?"

"That's right. Then, at the Mint, they test each shipment to find the value of each bar. They say the average bar of bullion is about one-quarter gold by weight to three-quarters silver. The Mint pays the mill owners based on what they receive. The mill owners get paid, subtract their cut, and the rest goes to the mining company. The company subtracts expenses, and investors back East collect a dividend."

"That's how I understand it works," Tilman said.

"Ought to work," Early corrected. "You see, the mining companies have a pretty good idea how much mineral should be in a ton of rock. The mill owners know what they process from the rock, and they have shipping manifests for how much bullion they say they load, but when it gets to the Mint, the manifest numbers don't match."

"And you're telling me this because . . ."

"Because somebody around here is doctoring the papers and getting to the bullion." Early nodded. "Just maybe somebody's holding up these stages and the bank to keep us from looking where we should, and maybe"—Early paused—"kinda double-dipping, you might say. Nobody seems to have much of a description about these bandits, do they? Except for a flower left behind. What kind of robbery is that? We're mighty curious."

"But some of these stagecoaches don't carry bullion." Tilman's mind raced with possibilities. "Unless . . ."

"What?"

"Unless they have bullion we don't know about, and nobody reports it missing." After a moment's silence Tilman sat back in his chair. "How do you know I'm not involved?"

"One of our deputies used to be a Pinkerton man, and he

knows a thing or two about inquiring into a man's character—what he is and what he was. He looked you over pretty close. He says you're on the square. Mind you"—Early took the match from his mouth and pointed it at Tilman—"if he's wrong, and you're on the take . . ." His eyes hardened. "Well, there ain't nothing I hate more than a crooked lawman. I'll see to it your pretty wife and those babies of yours will be visiting you behind bars for a long, long time."

"Your Pinkerton man's right about me. I can vouch for my deputy, Pegram, too," Tilman said. "Are you willing to work with us?"

"You'll know what we know," Early said. "I aim to bust this up, and I'll see you get credit as due." The two men sat looking out the window, each taking the other's measure.

"Wagner, what do you know about Prosper Charbonneau?" Early pulled out a knife and a small piece of wood and began to whittle on a whistle. He carefully worked over Tilman's wastebasket, but shavings still fell to the floor. "You know his past, I take it?"

"Yep. You should know he made some overtures to me when I became sheriff to see if I was willing to work with him. Subtle, but testing the water, so to speak." Tilman stopped. "He does business with Horace Tabor in Leadville and several of the important men in this Valley. Has a shady past, but then"—Tilman smiled—"so do I."

"He's the one I think might be worth watching. Hear he has his eye out to be an important man, and that mansion he's building on the other side of town testifies to that. He's got one daughter, and she's married to Jim Peel up in Granite. He sent her to relatives and a school in New Orleans for a time, probably trying to avoid her knowing about his business on the other side of the tracks."

Early stood, then turned to leave. "I 'preciate the help, Wagner, believe you me, and I'll be in touch." He closed his pocketknife and dropped it and the whistle into a coat pocket. After brushing wood shavings from his trousers into the trash and onto the floor, Early headed out the door.

Chapter Thirteen

Snow flurries in the early morning foretold an early winter, and the low cloud deck lingered still. A cold north wind moaned through the stands of ponderosa pine interspersed with aspen groves. The air smelled sharp and clean. Marie Fleur, wearing men's clothing and ready for excitement, looked for gold flakes in shallow, slow-moving Clear Creek high in the mountains about four miles southwest of Granite. "It's a great morning for an adventure, cousin, isn't it?"

"You are something else, Marie Fleur. You should have been a man. That would have kept your father busy, that's for sure."

Marie Fleur laughed aloud. Her breath, a small cloud of condensation in front of her face, delighted her. Marcel looked on in amusement. He loved Marie Fleur like the sister he'd never had, but he also felt sorry for Jim Peel. Life here would never come up to her expectations. Eventually her joy would give way to bitter disappointment, and she would become callous. However, for the moment she was merely a laughing young woman who knew no fear and threw caution to the wind.

Marcel kept watch on the irregular and rutted road that ran beside the creek. Higher in the west lay the mining towns of Vicksburg and Winfield. "Are you sure, cousin, that these men you brought are going to work out?" Marie Fleur called. "They can be trusted?"

Marcel removed his fancy gloves, stuffing them into the pockets of his duster, and came to join her by the creek. "Lars and Cooter Swenson have worked for me before. They owe their loyalty and their silence to the one who pays them. Their kind would rob you or kill you with as little concern as I might swat a fly. So, no, never trust them. When they're around, always wear your gun. If things ever go bad, they won't stick by us."

"Tell me why we need such men to ride with us." She tilted her head and regarded Marcel with obvious skepticism.

"The job I planned for today requires more than only we two."

"Yes, a stagecoach. But why can't we do it alone?"

Marcel should have told her before now. He had feared that Marie Fleur might balk at the idea of bringing in two men unknown to her to become a part of their new life of adventure. Patience and tact might win her over and ease any misgivings. "You and I will cover the driver and the shotgun guard and anyone riding on top. Lars and Cooter are here to cover the passengers who are riding inside so that we are not surprised."

"Very well, cousin." She pointed to the road. "Here they come now." Two men rode up, clearly glad to see Marcel waiting

Introductions made, Marie Fleur noted that the two brothers looked alike and were small in stature, the same way that she and Marcel were. In their coats, hats, gloves, and bandannas they would all look the same. That was a good thing. She liked the picture she saw in her mind. Four men, no distinguishing features. Marcel had planned well. She would keep an eye on these two, but they seemed manageable.

"So, Marcel. What are we going to do on this out-of-the-way road?" Cooter looked around. "I don't see nothing to rob. You sure you two need us?" He looked at Marie Fleur, not bothering to hide his interest. "This is some fine woman, Marcel. Your *cousin?*" He emphasized the word, doubt clearly reflected in his tone of voice.

"Watch your tone of voice, my friend." Cooter felt the edge of a knife blade press against his throat. Marie Fleur stood behind him, her anger barely in control. "I *am* his cousin. Have no doubt. Do you understand?"

"Just kidding, ma'am." Cooter touched his fingers to his throat, then looked at them to be sure he wasn't bleeding. "You're fast with that blade. I give you that."

"Okay." Marcel took over, trying to get their attention. "Listen up. Once a week the mines at Winfield and Vicksburg ship their gold dust to Granite for further shipment by rail to the Buena Vista smelter. They'll be coming down this road in a little while, and I figure we'll take the gold, rob the good folks in the stage, and send them on their way."

"That's it? Hah!" Marie Fleur turned and stormed away from Marcel and the others. She stopped, hands on hips, threw back her head, and laughed in disbelief. "You call that a plan?"

"What's wrong with it?" Marcel controlled his voice. He hated it when she turned her back on him. Worse, he hated that she had the audacity to question him in front of the two hired guns. Later, he would speak with her. He heard Cooter snicker, glad that he wasn't the only one to incur Marie Fleur's wrath.

She turned to face Marcel. "You're just going to ride out into the middle of the road from behind that boulder, and they will halt on your command? They will peacefully allow you to rob them?"

"When you and I ride out, you mean. We'll have our guns drawn. We take them by surprise. We'll get the drop on them, and they'll have no choice." Marcel spoke heatedly. "The boys will help us out as needed."

Lars stepped between the two. "I reckon it'll have to work. I hear the stage coming."

Minutes later Marie Fleur conceded that Marcel's plan was not as bad as she had thought. She and Marcel blocked the road and indeed stopped the two spans of mules pulling a canvas-topped celerity wagon of the kind used on Colorado's mountainous stage routes. At least there would be no passengers riding atop the cheerfully red-lacquered coach with yellow running gear. She held her raised pistol pointed at the stagecoach's driver. The shotgun messenger, his sawed-off shotgun tossed beside the road, sat with raised hands. Marcel covered the messenger. Several gawking passengers leaned out the leather-curtained open sides to see what was going on. They ignored orders to stay inside.

Marcel reined his horse to a halt beside one of the wheeler mules. "Throw down that strongbox."

The messenger turned his head and spat a stream of tobacco juice. "Can't do it."

"Can't or won't?" This was not what Marcel had expected. The messenger was supposed to be cowed during a robbery.

"Can't."

Marcel cocked his pistol and aimed at the messenger's face. "Why can't you?"

"Ain't got one. The strongbox went out yesterday."

Marcel edged his horse closer and stood in his stirrups to peer into the front boot under the man's feet.

When Marcel took his eyes off the messenger, the man grabbed for a pistol under his coat and swung it toward Marcel.

"Liar!" Marcel saw the strongbox at the same time the sudden and unexpected movement by the messenger alerted him to trouble. He snapped off a pistol shot but missed and spurred his horse to get out from under the man's gun.

Another shot rang out from the messenger's gun, the bullet harmlessly burying itself in the road. Two shots followed when Marie Fleur acted to save Marcel's life by shooting at the messenger. Her first shot went wild, but the second clipped the toe of the man's left brogan where his foot rested on the floorboard. Accurate shooting from the back of a horse was not something Jim had taught her. Before she could fire again, the messenger dropped his pistol and put his hands down to feel his ruined shoe and check if there was any blood. The bullet had ruined his brogan but cut no flesh. She'd have to practice that kind of shooting if they were going to rob stagecoaches.

"Enough!" the driver shouted. "You can have the box!" He wrestled it from the boot and heaved it onto the road. "You want the mail sacks too? They're in the back boot."

"No, I don't want the mail." Turning to Marie Fleur, Marcel called, "Keep 'em covered!" Dismounting, he fired a shot that broke the strongbox lock and quickly threw back the lid. Inside were four heavy cloth sausages fat with gold flakes and dust.

While Marcel transferred the gold sacks to his saddlebags, Lars and Cooter ordered the passengers to dismount and hand over their valuables. A stout but tightly corseted woman dressed in black wailed and cursed Lars as a "tief" and Cooter as a "vicked, vicked man" for robbing innocent, hardworking folk. Even so, Cooter emptied her purse without remorse.

When Marcel remounted, Lars and Cooter herded the passengers back inside. Then they quickly and expertly cut the team loose from the coach by simply disconnecting the doubletrees from the wagon shaft. To keep the mules from becoming entangled with the reins, Cooter used his sheath knife to cut them free. Lars slapped the wheeler mule's rump and shouted "H'up!" The mules, still harnessed, trotted off down the road and soon disappeared around a curve in the road.

The driver let fly a string of curses. "Hey, mister. How d'ya think we're supposed to get to town now you've run off our mules?"

"Why, you'll have to walk. And by the time you get to town, we'll be long gone." Cooter sneered.

Marie Fleur guided her horse to the now-empty strongbox and dropped a single flower inside. Spurring their horses, the gang followed the mules. Once out of sight of the stranded coach, Marcel uncovered his face and reined up. "All right, split up now. Boys, I'll be in touch with your cut of the gold."

"What about the passengers' money?" Marie Fleur tugged her bandanna from her face. She was not ready to give the other two any advantage in the take.

"Penny-ante stuff," Lars said. Quickly he went through the passenger take. It didn't take long. "Not enough for a good drunk on cheap whiskey."

Cooter snorted. "That old Dutch gal was good for only two dollars and some change! I hope you got enough from that box to pay better'n that."

"We got more. Now go and lay low. I'll send for you."

The two brothers nodded, spurred their horses, and headed for the saloon in Granite. They had enough of a haul to spend a day or two drinking until Marcel needed them again.

Chapter Fourteen

Butter wrapped a rag around the handle of the pot of boiling coffee and slid it to the back of the stove. He flipped open the lid and added a cup of cold water to settle the grounds. He poured two cups of the scalding brew, passing one to Tilman. Both men savored the coffee in silence.

Home these days was a sight different from when they first met and were each by themselves. Now *home* meant the sound of babies, wives cooking and talking, laughter, love, and sorrow. Although it was wonderful, there remained little time for silence.

Tilman drained his cup before he spoke. "Say, old man, weren't you supposed to wait for the grinds to settle?"

"They settle while you're talking," Butter answered.

"But I wasn't talking."

"Well, go on with what you were gonna say about that Marshal Early."

Tilman had gone over the reason for Tom Early's visit, and Butter was clearly anxious to know the outcome. "Early runs a string of spies, and one of 'em says there's talk about 'the gang' lifting a gold shipment from Leadville when the train stops to take on water at Granite Station."

"What shipment and what 'gang'?"

"Haw Tabor's shipment. He's moving a good-sized box of placer dust he collected from prospectors he's grubstaked— you know how he's always done that—and since he likes for everybody to know how well he's doing, he talks it up. I don't know for sure about the gang. They may be the ones who robbed the bank here in town. Early thinks they're probably responsible for shooting up the stage between Winfield and Balltown up by Twin Lakes. Didn't hurt anybody. Ran the team off and left the passengers sitting until the company realized they were late and sent help."

"At Winfield they shot at the express rider," Butter said, "and he's an old friend of mine. But they did empty the strong-box and left a flower in it when they skedaddled. Darnedest thing I ever heard."

"We're going to ride up and talk to Jim Peel. He's the town marshal at Granite. We'll ask him to help us. We'll see if we can be there to welcome whoever tries to hold up that train."

"I know Peel. Met him when he used to be sheriff," Butter said. "I hear he's been drinking a lot. Guess he expected to be county sheriff, not Purdy. Must've taken somethin' out of him. You sure you can trust him?"

"One way to find out," Tilman answered.

Chapter Fifteen

Butter reined up in front of the saloon, then swung down from the saddle to dab the reins over the rail. He stretched. "I'd better start bringing a piller to sit on, Tilman. My back-side is starting to feel all this riding here and there since you got to be the sheriff."

Tilman tried not to smile as he dismounted from the horse he'd hired from the livery. "Quit your grumpin, ol' man. Be glad we caught the train up here today. Lot shorter ride from the stables than all the way from Buena Vista." Tilman looked at the weather-grayed building. It had been hastily thrown up during the boom times using green, unseasoned wood never touched by a drop of paint. Now ever-widening gaps between warped boards got worse with each passing year. "Don't know why this saloon hasn't collapsed. It looked bad when I met Bat Masterson here when I first came to Colorado a few years back."

"Looking for Dan's killer. I recollect that time."

Tilman reflected on the memory. "The papers say Masterson not only works as Creede's town marshal, but he also runs a local gambling establishment."

"I heard that too, Tilman. However"—Butter looked up and down the empty street of mostly boarded-up buildings—"I also hear he wears a lavender corduroy suit. Must look plumb fancy!"

The two men laughed.

"Mind, you," Butter continued, "I wouldn't tell him to his face, but I can't imagine a lavender corduroy suit on a man. Can you?"

A narrow drainage ditch fed by melt water and seeps uphill from the saloon crossed the rutted dirt road. "I never would have believed hard times would hit Granite like this." Patches of dirty snow lingered in the shadows of buildings. "Funny thing, I'm back in the same town, same saloon, hunting for somebody who broke the law, same as before." The trickle of water in the ditch ran clear, and the wet gravel sparkled with flecks of minerals that looked liked silver and gold but were mainly fool's gold and mica. "I keep meaning to bring me a pan, a pick, and a shovel and come up here and do some prospecting."

"When do you think you're going to have time for prospecting for gold, Tilman? When those twins are in school?"

"Quit your yapping, Butter. You're worse than a woman." He looked around one last time, then started for the saloon. "Let's get it done."

"Peel will be fine. Everything I've ever heard about him says he's a good man. The business with the bottle, well, I figure he's just had one disappointment too many."

They went through the door into the single long, dimly lit room that was the saloon. A roughhewn bar ran down one side. There was no back door. Two dirty windows across from the bar let in some daylight, and oil lanterns struggled to overcome the shadows. The air inside told of years of tobacco and lamp-oil smoke, spit, spilled beer, whiskey, and blood soaked into the walls and floors. Tables were scattered around, several occupied, some with one man in his cups, and others with two or three men. Tilman noticed cards, but mostly the men drank. The little talk among them halted when the strangers came in. Men saw Tilman's badge and the belted pistol under his coat but avoided the lawman's gaze. Slowly conversation resumed.

The bartender wiped down the bar. "What'll it be, gents?"

Tilman shook his head, eyes narrowed. Hard memories came to mind. The last time he'd walked into this saloon, he saw a man gunned down not ten feet from where he now stood. He scanned the room for Jim Peel.

Out of habit Butter stood so that he could see the door and cover Tilman's back. But he was not about to let go of his ideas about Bat Masterson. "Come to think of it, Marcel Devereaux looks a lot like Bat used to look. He wears those dandy suits and has a black bowler hat. I've seen Marcel in it when he's at work for Charbonneau. That Marcel fellow even wears fancy leather gloves with his initial on them. Heard he orders them special from New Orleans."

"I reckon you're right." Tilman spotted Jim in the shadows sitting at a rear corner table. He elbowed Butter and nodded at Peel. A pistol, a nearly empty bottle of whiskey, and one glass were on the table. Jim, his head buried in his hands, had not seen Tilman and Butter.

"Some sorry-looking town marshal you make, Jim Peel!" Tilman picked the bottle up and tossed it to Butter, who caught it and set it on an empty table.

"What?" Peel fumbled drunkenly for his gun on the table but knocked it to the floor instead. Tilman scooped up the pistol. He and Butter sat across from a downcast Jim.

"How long you been sitting here?" Butter sniffed. "Ugh. I don't know what smells worse, you or this place," Butter chided Peel, who looked around and raised a hand to signal for another drink. The bartender started to bring over a fresh bottle, but Tilman stopped him, motioning him to the far end of the bar.

"Aw, why'd you do that?"

The barman returned with three mugs and a pot of coffee.

Butter spoke to Peel. "You remember Sheriff Wagner. Knowed him for a long time, and I can vouch for him."

Peel stared first at Butter, then at Tilman, nodded, and looked up as the bartender poured the coffee.

"You're in luck. Just brewed this fresh around noon, so it still has some taste to it."

The men didn't comment. They waited until Jim had downed the coffee. Satisfied he wasn't going to start anything, Butter ordered a beer instead of coffee. The bartender drew a schooner of Stumpf's Pueblo Lager and walked over to set it in front of Butter. "In case you boys don't know it, Jim's been around for quite a few years. He's a good man, but losing the election really changed him. He's taken to that bottle in a big way."

Tilman nodded, and the bartender left. In the next fifteen minutes Butter refilled their coffee mugs several times, chattering about nothing as only Butter could while nursing his beer. Butter talked until Jim finally put his hands up in protest. "If you don't quit, I'm going to float away. Pegram, where did you learn so many words?"

"We need your help, Peel, and you can't do it tied to a bottle." Tilman looked around and, seeing that the saloon was now mainly empty, leaned into the table. "Are you going to drink your life away, or can you remember you're a lawman sworn to uphold the law in this town?"

Jim looked at Tilman through bloodshot eyes, anger slowly rising in them. "Whoa. Just hold on there, Wagner." He shoved back his chair to stand but then seemed to realized that he was still much too woozy. He fell back into his seat. "What do you know about anything?"

"I know more than you think. I know you wanted the job Oliver Purdy got. And you think it should have been yours after he died. People say you and Prosper Charbonneau had an understanding of some kind, and the election finished that deal. How'd you like to start all over?"

"What are you getting at?"

"I'm in this job only until the next election."

"Okay. I get you now. But . . ." Jim sat up straighter, starting to look alive again. "Hey, Prosper and I didn't have any agreement. Be clear on that. I married Marie because I love her. I don't know what he planned, but I wasn't ever asked about anything else. Get that straight. Get this too. You're right about me resenting your taking that job. I know you didn't go ask for it, but I still resent it. That's how small I am." Jim stared at the bottle on the nearby table. He looked back at Tilman.

To Tilman's way of thinking, this Peel was all set to wallow in self-pity for the rest of his life. "I gave up using my gun, and I was right content with running my spread and trying to do right by my wife and kids. This wasn't my idea, Jim, but somebody had to do it. Unless you climb out of that bottle," Tilman goaded, "you'll never be man enough to handle it."

Jim lurched from his chair to throw a jab at Tilman's jaw.

Tilman easily pushed the drunk's punch aside, kicking Jim's feet from under him, spilling him to the floor.

Tilman looked down at the man. "Are you ready to start over?"

Jim looked at the floor, then raised his eyes to Tilman. "I got no place else to go but up. Yeah, I'm ready."

Tilman extended his hand.

"Well, I hate to interrupt this championship bare-knuckle brawl you two fellas got goin', but we ain't got time for you to go the next twenty rounds. I think we came up here to do a job." Butter grinned as he studied the two men. He loved to stir the pot. Oh, yes, indeed.

Seeing that there'd be no fight, the other men in the saloon turned back to their drinks.

"Be quiet, Butter." Tilman turned to Jim and pulled him to his feet. "I'm asking you point-blank, Peel. How deep are you in Prosper's pocket, and are you with us or against us? I need to know. I need help, but I want to know my back is covered, not being aimed at."

Jim thought for a minute, obviously working out his answer. "Prosper doesn't have much need for me now, if he ever did. If you and Butter are willing to give me a chance, I think I can remember what I used to believe in and try to make this right again." He shook Tilman's hand and turned to Butter as well. "Now, what do you two need?"

They sat. In a quiet voice Tilman said, "We heard that Horace Tabor will be shipping gold bars through here on the train. If we know that, then chances are good that this 'Flower Gang' knows as well and may be planning to lift it. We think Granite is where it's going to happen. It's supposed to be coming through next week, on Thursday. We need you to keep a close eye, and we'll take the stage the day before from Buena Vista so we can work together. That way, if we're right, maybe we can stop these people for good."

"I'll keep an eye out here and check around. I know a couple of men who would sell their souls for a drink." Jim smiled as he looked at his empty glass. "Guess I'm a fine one to talk. Still, they'll do to stand with us, and you can put up at the hotel."

"Peel, they all make a mistake sooner or later. It wouldn't hurt your reputation if you were in on the capture."

"I reckon I can help you out, Wagner. Thanks for giving me a chance."

Outside, the sun was sliding behind the mountains, and the air was cooling down fast. When they boarded the train and left Granite, Butter looked around at the row of houses and the shadows the mountains threw across the valley. "What a place. Too raw for me. Always thought so, even when I was driving for the mines."

Tilman agreed, content to let Butter fill the evening quiet. "A place like this could drive a man to drink."

Chapter Sixteen

Fifty thousand dollars, sir!" Tilman looked up as a man stormed into the office cussing. "Fifty thousand dollars taken in broad daylight off the stage!"

"Whoa! Whoa! Whoa there!" Tilman pushed back his chair and came around his desk. He was not one to take a cussing from anybody. "You got a beef with me, you'd best watch your mouth and tell me who the devil you—" Tilman stopped to look at the man more closely. He was richly dressed, of medium height, and balding with a wide mustache. But something about the man jogged his memory. It was the cold, pale eyes. "You're Tabor. Horace Tabor."

Taken aback, the man cocked his head and stared at Tilman. "I am, but have we met, sir?"

"I'm Tilman Wagner. Five or six years back. I was staying at Zebulon Mansfield's hotel up at Twin Lakes, and you came down from Leadville. You were ridin' high after a big strike and doing some celebrating."

"Name doesn't ring a bell," Tabor said. "I can't place you."

"We didn't exactly hit it off back then, either," Tilman said. "Now, let's sit down and talk."

Tabor, face livid and hands shaking, sat. "That was my shipment the highwaymen took off that stage—fifty thousand in gold dust and flakes, it was. What kind of protection does the law provide in this county? Pretty sorry, in my opinion. What are you doing to apprehend those people and get it back?"

Tabor stood, paced the room, and sat back down again, trying to control his temper.

"Look here, Tabor. You never told me you were shipping anything out of the ordinary. I found out about a gold shipment from a third-hand tip-off. When I asked your agent in Granite, he told me the box was shipping by train from the station there in Granite. Does he not speak for you?"

"Yes, yes. But that was a ploy." Tabor was calming down. "There've been so many robberies, I said we should let slip that the shipment was going by train and instead put it aboard the stage, and if the robbers hit the train, they'd come away empty-handed, and my shipment would be safe."

"Well, that beats all!"

"I've let slip the wrong information before, and it always worked."

"Well, it didn't this time, and I can only take that to mean that somebody knew the real story." Tilman looked at Tabor. "Wouldn't you agree?"

Tabor sat still, obviously thinking about what Tilman had said. "But who?"

"I'd guess someone who works for you overheard you talking or figured out that the gold seemed to be headed in a different direction. I don't know, Tabor. It's your operation, but how in blazes do you expect us to help when you don't even give us the right information?"

"I don't guess I can expect you to." Tabor stood and made to leave. "Sheriff Wagner, I'll see to this myself. I have an idea or two, and I'll look and see what I can find out myself."

Tabor stepped out of the building, pulling his fur collar closer to his chin, and climbed into a waiting carriage. He reached out and tapped for his driver. "Take me to Charbonneau's place." He'd get to the bottom of this. Action—that's how Tabor worked. Prosper was a two-bit conniver, and he'd better not be up to anything, or Tabor would have him taken care of real quick.

Chapter Seventeen

W hat is the matter, Haw honey?" Baby Doe looked in alarm as Tabor stewed on the carriage seat beside her, urging their driver to hurry. She moved closer, her brow wrinkling with concern, wondering what had her husband so irritated. The faint, heady fragrance of expensive perfume filled the opulent coach as she took a silk handkerchief and dabbed her husband's brow. "You need to take a deep breath." She carried on, glancing out the window at Buena Vista to see if anyone noticed their passage. She liked to be noticed. Her small hand gently patted Tabor on the arm. To console him, she whispered into his ear, "It's only money, dear. We have loads."

Tabor turned to look at Baby Doe's small face and burst out laughing. "By gum, Baby, you do take all." He hugged her close to him. "Augusta would have my head for this." He laughed all the way down Main Street while Baby Doe smiled to herself. She might not be as smart as Tabor's first wife, but she knew a sight more about how to handle a man, especially Horace Tabor.

Prosper Charbonneau's town office rooms above the First Carbonate National Bank had been designed with care and reflected elegance and good taste. He'd hired a designer from Denver to come down and "do it up right." The walls were painted deep gold, and the furniture was ornate. Overstuffed leather chairs surrounded a small gilt table, and fresh flowers adorned a short Greek column in the center of the room. Prosper had paid dearly for the effect, but felt it worth every penny.

He stood at the top of the stairs by the entryway, watching

as the Tabors got out of the carriage. Prosper stared in fascination, admiring the soft femininity of Baby Doe as a small foot daintily felt for the ground. He gazed at her tangled mass of curls and pouty lips. Baby Doe might be worth the grief Tabor had faced for leaving his wife Augusta. Prosper felt a moment's regret that he was alone, but only for a moment. He liked the life he led, and a wife didn't fit into it at this time. Maybe one day, but not now.

Charbonneau saw that Tabor was tending to fat, and he had a ruddy complexion that seemed to get worse with each year. Still, Prosper knew that he was a man to reckon with, and so he tried to stay on his good side.

When Tabor left Augusta for Baby Doe, the whole of Colorado had seemed to reel from the blow. Augusta was constant and reliable but dull, like a slice of bread. Baby Doe was fine wine, the sunshine, and all other things a man desired. Tabor didn't care about the talk. He and Augusta had worked hard side by side, and he had struggled as an average businessman trying to hold things together. He had gambled a small amount on a mine others said was worthless, but it had been the right move. Overnight he became one of the richest men in Colorado. From what Prosper had heard, Augusta had mistrusted the sudden money, shunned the fancy clothes, and the rift between the spouses had continued to widen, and when Horace met Baby Doe, that was that. Prosper knew she was at least twenty-something years younger than Tabor, but it didn't seem to bother them. They married after a huge and public row with Augusta.

Prosper hadn't been invited to the wedding, but he had heard it was a garish affair, and many people had laughed about it behind Tabor's back. He watched Tabor help Baby Doe across a pothole in the street and noted that Horace seemed as entranced by her as usual.

"Well, Haw, Baby Doe. Good to see you." Prosper greeted the two as they climbed to the top of the steps. "Let's go into my office, Haw, and get the business out of the way. Baby Doe, you look lovely as always. I'll have my secretary, Mr. Henders, get you one of the new fashion books I keep for the ladies while I talk with their husbands." He motioned to Henders and closed the door to his inner office.

"What is going on, Charbonneau?" Tabor dropped his calm demeanor, tossing his hat onto the hat stand by Prosper's desk.

"I don't know, Haw. I was as surprised as you. None of my boys had any wind of a robbery."

"I don't understand. I had the word out on the streets that we were going through Granite. Apparently that new sheriff of yours did his job too well, and he was there, all right, but where were the crooks?" Tabor paced, not noticing Prosper's new mahogany desk.

"Wagner pays attention. I give him that. He had my son-in-law, Jim Peel, and some other men ready but for nothing." Prosper paused, weighing his words. "It is almost as if the robbers knew this was fake." He continued. "Course, that can't be unless you have a spy in your employ."

"Me!" Tabor fumed. "Me! You're the only one around here who could pull off something like this, I figure. Are you trying to double-cross me? I give you plenty. What more do you want, Prosper?"

"I'm flattered and hurt, Haw. I'm fine with our arrangement. I've done nothing you don't know about. I think that someone who works for you must be letting this gang of thieves in on what's happening." Prosper opened his liquor cabinet and poured Haw a whiskey and one for himself.

There was little trust between the two men, but each needed the other. Prosper took one of his fine Havana cigars and offered Tabor one.

"You may be right, Prosper. But I don't know where to start to look."

The two men finished their cigars and whiskey without finding an answer to their problem. Soon they came out to join Baby Doe, only to find she had company already. Marie Fleur sat beside the new Mrs. Tabor as they chatted over a recent Goody's magazine that Prosper kept in the waiting room for the occasional woman visitor. It was one of Marie's ideas that paid off with the ladies.

Baby Doe was up in a flash, the magazine falling to the floor as she took Tabor's arm while Marie Fleur retrieved the magazine. "We were admiring the newest fashions in this wonderful magazine."

Prosper could not help but see the contrast between the two women. Of average height, Marie Fleur had skin of ivory, and her raven hair gave tell to the French blood she carried. Dark red lips and eyes as black as night made her a woman men noticed. While she was not a traditional beauty, or soft like Baby Doe, she possessed an air of mystery and barely contained energy that drew men. Today she wore a deep garnet travel suit that featured a soft gray trim and bustle.

Haw Tabor acknowledged Marie Fleur.

"Mr. Tabor. I believe we met, but I was much younger then."

"I remember. You have turned into a lovely young woman." Haw turned to Prosper. "I am sure you're proud of your daughter."

Baby Doe moved a little closer to her husband. It never hurt to show who belonged where. Marie Fleur was beautiful, but she wasn't Tabor's type. He liked a small, helpless woman. Marie Fleur wasn't tall, but there was nothing soft about her.

"Yes, I only wish I got to see her more often. She and that husband of hers stay in Granite most of the time."

The Tabors chatted for a moment and then stepped out into the brisk afternoon. "Hope I make it back down these danged stairs in one piece," Horace grumbled.

Prosper followed the two down the stairs, and Tabor continued to chat as he and Baby Doe got into the carriage to catch the afternoon train to return to Leadville.

Horace leaned out the window as they departed. "I'll get back to you, Prosper, on the matter we discussed. You look into it on your side."

"Will do, Haw. You and the missus stay safe."

"What brings you here, Marie Fleur?" Prosper joined his daughter back in his office.

"Are the things they say about Tabor's new wife the truth?" Marie Fleur watched as the carriage drove away.

"What things?"

"I hear she spends money as if there is no tomorrow. I hear

there is another husband someplace around Carson City maybe. I hear that Augusta was the steel behind that fortune and that Haw Tabor just got lucky and struck it rich and then left her for young Mrs. Tabor, even though Augusta didn't want him to leave. I heard . . ."

"Marie Fleur. No more, please. I'm sorry I asked. It isn't our business. He is a business acquaintance, and that is all. His private life is his own." Prosper got his hat and cane. "Come on, daughter, and I'll treat you to lunch at the hotel." He turned to her. "If you promise not to ask any more questions."

Chapter Eighteen

Tilman thought of Paul Fry, the circuit-riding preacher, as a good friend as well as his pastor. When Tilman and Catherine were in New Mexico, Pastor Fry had married Minna, the widow who owned the land on the northern border of Catherine and Tilman's place. He still rode circuit but was in Buena Vista more and more now that a church had been built. Several people from the neighboring towns came to Buena Vista to attend services, and Paul welcomed Pastor Whipple in the summer to share the load. Soon Whipple would take the outlying communities, and Paul would serve only in Buena Vista.

After supper, Catherine excused herself, while the two men moved to sit on the front porch, where Paul could indulge his sole remaining vice—a good smoke. Paul talked at length, comparing Denver's electric lights to Leadville's, and in his opinion Leadville's was far and away the better system. As he talked, he fished a cigar from an inside pocket of his coat, held it under his nose, and sniffed it appreciatively. He paused, studied the tobacco, bit off the closed end and spat it over the rail, and then from another pocket produced a match. With a thumbnail he scratched the match head, which flared in the darkness. With audible puffs he soon had a good burn going, and he settled back in his rocker.

Lamplight from the parlor window silhouetted Paul. Tilman watched him as he leaned his head back and sent a perfectly circular smoke ring toward the ceiling, only to see it drift away on the gentle evening breeze. Tilman puzzled over his friend's behavior. "What's bothering you? You got something on your mind?"

Paul leaned forward in his chair, elbows resting on his knees, and studied Tilman. "I do, and that's a fact."

Silence ensued, and finally Tilman couldn't stand the wait. "Well, are you going to tell me what it is?"

More silence. Paul leaned back and began rocking slowly to and fro. "There's talk in Denver about that gang of highwaymen been deviling you hereabouts, the ones that leave a flower."

Paul's words touched a sore spot, spurring Tilman's sharp response. "What kind of talk?"

Paul suppressed a smile at Tilman's irritation. "Kind of like they're some kind of heroes, stealing from the big digs, not bothering the little man."

"Now, look here . . ." Tilman stood and walked to the end of the porch, where he bent to put his hands on the rail in thought. He looked over his shoulder at Paul. "They're thieves, pure and simple. Smart, yes, able to get away with it, yes, so far, but they'll make a mistake, and I'll get 'em." Tilman faced Paul. "Besides, they robbed a stagecoach just the other day and left the poor folks stranded on the road till the stage company missed them and came to find them. What's heroic about that?"

"Are you getting close?" Paul asked.

Tilman returned to his seat with a resigned sigh. "No, not even. Anyway, Fry, what is this flower nonsense? I think they're making fun of us all."

Paul had expected Tilman's answer and was quick to ask, "Well, why don't you use me?"

"What?" Tilman didn't believe he'd heard that right.

"Use me. I get around and hear things. You forget I used to ride a different trail before I became a preacher. Talk to me, tell me what you know, and maybe I can see things from a different point of view, maybe ask a good question or two. I might think of something you've overlooked."

Tilman shook his head, certain that Paul Fry had gone crazy to suggest such a thing. "Is the mountain air finally getting to you, or have you gone off the wagon?"

"Hah!" The cigar end glowed brightly as Paul spewed clouds of smoke, grinning at Tilman's consternation. "Neither, and you know it."

"Fine. I'll think about it. That's the best I can do for now."

Paul took the cigar from his mouth and spat over the rail. Whenever he smoked a stogie, he habitually chewed the end until it unraveled wetly. He claimed he got double for his money, for to him it was satisfying to have a "chaw" and a "smoke" at the same time. He tossed the butt into the yard, rose from the chair, and stretched. "Better start for home. Minna will be wondering where I am if I don't get home soon."

Tilman kicked off his boots, leaned back in his chair, stretched his legs, and put his feet up on the porch rail. He wiggled his toes. "Yep. I'm tired myself, and those twins love to sing a little song around daybreak most days."

"Thank goodness I'm just their godfather." Paul laughed. "They're cute little rascals, though."

Tilman bade his friend a good night. He had to admit, Paul's idea was not as far-fetched as it first appeared. He was a man of many facets, and he was definitely not one of those Sunday-only-Bible-thumping-brotherly-love-please-pass-the-fried-chicken kind of preachers you wouldn't trust to be alone with your sister. He'd been over the mountain, and his mind was sharp. As he sat alone in the quiet darkness with his thoughts, Tilman had the distinct feeling he'd just been buffaloed.

Tilman had left orders with the clerks that once he closed his office door, he was going to be busy and didn't want to be bothered. He leaned back in his chair, feet resting on the opened bottom drawer of his desk, ankles crossed. It felt good to take it easy for a minute.

Since assuming the job of sheriff, he'd had to contend with the usual drunks and a couple of minor saloon fights. Things had gotten pretty exciting when a love-struck freight-wagon driver stabbed a miner in a fight over one of the girls at Peg Leg Sal's so-called boardinghouse for young women, but the day-to-day routine of his work was just that: routine. But the antics of the gang of robbers, growing bolder by the week, it seemed, was something he couldn't figure. He needed some fresh ideas, and after some thought he'd decided to take Paul Fry's offer. So he'd asked Tom Early to come by to talk. He'd also asked Pastor Paul Fry to sit in, because the man was right. He might bring a fresh perspective to the problem.

Tilman listened as Butter regaled Tom Early with a story from his stagecoach-driving days.

"You ready to start?" Early interrupted Butter to ask Tilman. He was clearly not interested in the story.

"Here he comes now," Tilman said as Pastor Paul Fry walked into the room.

After being introduced to Fry, Early looked askance at Tilman. "Pastor? You mean a preacher's part of this?"

"You're right on both counts," Tilman answered. "You'd be surprised how he gets around the Valley and who he knows. Don't let that undertaker's suit fool you. He wasn't always a preacher."

"That's right," Butter said. "Back in the day he was a Yankee cavalryman ridin' with Phil Sheridan—one of them skinny youngsters, a bachelor not a-scared of anything or anybody, the kind Sheridan asked for when he took over with Grant."

Patting a growing paunch, Fry said to Early, "I was a few pounds younger then!"

His joke was lost on Early. The man had never had much humor, and what little there was had been rubbed off in the years he'd worked in the raw Colorado mining camps. "C'mon, let's get on with this."

"I'll just listen," Fry said, taking a seat. "You go ahead."

Tilman opened the discussion by reviewing the few bits of information they had to go on. He guessed that the bank robbery in Buena Vista, the robbery of the messenger south of town, and the stage holdup outside Granite were likely all done by the same gang. The robbers had brandished rifles and pistols, but no one was shot in any of the three robberies. In at least two cases a flower was left on the scene—he'd never heard whether they'd left one with the messenger. The "Flower Gang" made a respectable haul in each case, with the messenger losing the least, twelve thousand dollars, and Tabor claiming he lost over fifty thousand on the stage. The bank had never reported an exact figure in the loss, and when Tom Early snorted a suspicious laugh, Tilman admitted that there might be some-thing going on there worth looking into.

"Folks on the stage say there were four of them, all wearing long dusters, hats, and gloves, and their faces were covered by bandannas," Butter said. "The two in the bank dressed the same way, and they say the messenger saw only two."

"Did we hear anything else?" Early asked. "Anybody real tall or real short? Was one of 'em a fatty or maybe a beanpole?"

"Nobody said," Butter answered.

"How'd they happen to hit that particular stage, and did they know it would have a small fortune of Tabor's gold on it on that day?" Fry asked.

"Somebody in the know had to tell 'em," Tilman said. "Or it could have been pure, blind luck."

"How'd you happen to be in Granite waiting for the gang?" Fry asked.

"In this case, we got a tip, but Tabor decided to pull a switch and reroute the shipment. We didn't hear about it until it was over and done with," Tilman explained. "We came off looking like fools in the wrong place at the wrong time."

"There've been several robberies the last two months just outside of town here," Fry stated. "The one happened while we were at a church social."

"That's right. We looked on the road to Salida but didn't find anything except an empty bag. Hard to trace," Butter said.

"What about that young man, Charbonneau's nephew?"

"Marcel Devereaux's his name, and he's fairly new to town. Grew up in New Orleans, and rumor has it his mama sent him here, hoping he'd learn a trade from his uncle." Fry contributed that information.

"He's supposed to be helping in the business, ain't he?" Butter asked. "I see him and Prosper together around town."

Tilman swung his feet from the desk drawer to the floor and sat up in his chair, an idea forming in his mind. "Would Mar-cel know about Tabor's shipment? Tabor and Charbonneau do business."

Butter shrugged. "I don't know the answer to that."

"What do you know about this Marcel?" Early asked. "Is he

who he says? Where'd he come from? What did he do before he came here?"

"I can help you there," Butter said. "There's been bar talk about some gambling scrape over in Tin Cup, as well as a few other places. Might be worth looking into that."

"I can't act on any hearsay. One way to get to the facts of the matter," Tilman said, "is, I'll ride over there and ask around."

"I'll go along," Butter said.

"No need for that, old man."

"I'll side you," Butter insisted.

"Who'll mind things here if you both go?" Early asked.

"Deputize Peel," Fry suggested. "He's Charbonneau's son-in-law, but he spends a lot of time in town anyway."

Chapter Nineteen

Granite town marshal Jim Peel sat in a ladder-back chair leaning against the front wall of his office, enjoying the warmth of the day. He called it an office. Actually it was a dugout cut into the side of a hill, log-sided, with a leaky roof. It wasn't like his office in the old courthouse before Buena Vista stole the county seat. That was back when he was the county sheriff, when he was *somebody*. How far the mighty had fallen. "Humph," he snorted. Now, the courthouse had been torn down, its lumber sold to be used mostly to build head frames at two mines, a couple of shanties, and the leftovers went to board up a tent saloon.

The mining boom for Granite had gone bust, and a lot of the population had pulled up stakes and drifted for the new boomtowns. The few remaining die-hard miners made do panning river gravel in small claims, hoping for a little color and an occasional nugget. Several were reworking spoils from once-productive mines. The town residents lucky enough to manage a decent living for their families were railroad workers at the station, the men who worked for the stagecoach lines, and, as always, the saloon keepers. The operator of the general store was considered well off. Of course, as town marshal, Peel did all right supporting Marie on his fifty-dollars-a-month salary. He'd hoped to do better by her, for she was accustomed to finer things than he could provide. That was probably the reason she was spending more time away from home, visiting her father down the Valley in Buena Vista.

A shouted greeting interrupted his thoughts. A boy made

his way up the washed-out gravel road toward him. It was the railroad telegrapher's son, a skinny boy about ten years old.

The boy stopped in front of Peel and rolled a lump from one cheek to the other before he spat a squirt of tobacco juice into the dirt. "Telegram come for you, Marshal." He reached a dirty hand into the canvas dispatch case slung by a strap over one shoulder and produced an envelope, which he handed to Peel. "Want me to read it for you?"

"No need. I can do it." Peel dug a coin from his vest pocket and thumbed a dime into the air.

The boy's hand snaked out to catch the coin. "Thanks. Be seein' you." He turned and headed down the hill as Peel opened the envelope.

After supper that night, Peel tossed his napkin onto the table and pushed his chair back so he could cross his legs while he drank his coffee. He'd never get used to Marie's coffee. She made a thick brew, heavy on the chicory, and insisted he drink it laced with cream and sugar. Truth be told, she wasn't much of a cook, either. From somewhere he had the notion that people from New Orleans were just naturally good cooks. He watched her take a pan of hot water from the laundry stove in the mudroom and pour it into a dishpan to wash the dishes. She was a beautiful woman, graceful, with wonderful, full-bodied curves beneath the apron she wore. Did she regret marrying him?

"Got a telegram today," he told her.

She wiped her hands dry on a dish towel. "Who was it from?"

Peel took out the paper and unfolded it. He laid it on the table. "From Sheriff Wagner."

As far as Marie Fleur knew, her husband had never received a telegram from the sheriff. "What does it say?"

"He wants to deputize me."

Marie Fleur came and sat in her chair across the table from him. She placed her elbows on the table and rested her chin in the palms of her hands. Clearly, her curiosity was piqued. "Why would he do that?"

"He said he'd be away from the office for a week, but he didn't say where. He needs someone to take care of things, and he knows I can do the job."

Marie Fleur took his empty coffee cup and saucer, added sugar, and half filled the cup with cream before adding coffee. She placed the cup in front of him. "How can he simply go away? Do the robbers not bedevil him? They do their work under his very nose, yet he cannot catch them." She laughed. "Poor man. People talk. He is becoming a laughingstock. Soon the people are going to be tired of this gang, and then the sheriff may not be so special anymore." She came behind Jim and leaned over his shoulder to hug him, her long hair spilling down over the side of his face. Jim breathed in a faint fragrance of roses. She hardly ever wore her hair down anymore; he had forgotten how it looked like a mysterious veil. When they first married, he used to tease her and call her his "woman of mystery." That was long ago.

He realized she was speaking to him.

"What did you say, Marie?"

"I said they might look to you then, like they should have done before Purdy."

She's right, Peel thought. He sipped the coffee, then returned the delicate cup to its saucer. "He didn't say much in the telegram. I expect he'll be on county business. Likely he knows something and wants to go learn more, or it could be he's going looking for somebody. Maybe it's part of the business with the robbers. He'll tell me if he wants me to know." He was quiet for a moment. "Wagner's an odd bird. He's honorable, though. Never rubs it in that he's sheriff and not me. Acts surprised they asked him. Seems likeable enough, but you never know what's going on in his mind. People say he rode a rough trail in Texas and down below Santa Fe. There's a hard man, I reckon. I'd hate to cross him."

"*Bien.* I will come with you. While you work, I shall visit my father. It will be like old times—you, the sheriff, and I, your dutiful wife."

Later, lying awake in bed with Marie asleep beside him, the wind moaning around the eaves of the house, Peel was uneasy.

Like old times, she'd said after supper. When she'd said that, had he heard a sharp edge of contempt in her voice? Was she quick, maybe too quick, to declare she'd go along and visit her papa? What was the attraction Buena Vista held for her? Another man? Was there someone else? His stomach started hurting as it always did when he worried. And, lately, he worried a lot. A drink would help.

Chapter Twenty

Tilman settled into the seat cushion of the oversized wooden armchair behind his desk. Oliver Purdy had bought it with his own money and had it shipped in from Denver. It was a pedestal chair with rollers on each foot. Jim Peel sat across the desk from him. "I take it nobody in Granite objected to your coming here?"

"No, things have been quiet lately."

"D'you think you can handle this job for me for a week or so while me and my deputy go to Tin Cup and look around?"

Tin Cup? Peel remained outwardly calm, but the sheriff's mention of Tin Cup got his attention. "Sure. What's in Tin Cup, Wagner?"

Tilman continued. "I'm getting there. What do you know about Prosper Charbonneau's nephew, Marcel Devereaux?"

Tilman saw the fleeting look of surprise that crossed Jim's face.

Jim Peel quickly regained his composure. "Marcel doesn't talk much to me. He and Marie are close, though. They grew up as close as brother and sister, since she lived with his family in New Orleans while she was young and going to school.

"But Marie says Marcel came here because he gambles. I gather he was a lousy gambler. Lost most of the time, and his family had to bail him out. His mother is Prosper's sister, and she sent him here hoping his uncle could straighten him out. Way I hear it, he's been slipping off and hitting the tables at Leadville, and, as usual, he's losing. I heard the boys up there were badgering him for their money, but that was a while back. I've heard nothing lately."

Tilman nodded. "I got a tip from another lawman that Devereaux had money trouble in Tin Cup as well. He kept company with a woman over there, a saloon gal, and she wanted to get married. He didn't. He left her, and she might be just mad enough to say something that might help us find out a little more."

Jim absentmindedly pulled a half-smoked cigar from his coat pocket, thumbed a match, and lit it. He liked an occasional good cigar but on his meager salary couldn't afford to throw away a butt unless he'd smoked it down to the least little stub he could hold. It hurt his pride for anyone to know that, and Tilman Wagner would never have seen that side of him if he hadn't been taken unaware by the questions about Marcel. "Why are you interested in Marcel?"

"Just looking at the newcomers in town. Marcel came here not too long before the robberies began. He dresses like a swell and lives pretty high, although Prosper has never been known as a generous employer, so I thought I'd take a look." Tilman sat back. "Probably nothing to this, but I thought it best to see if there's anything to it or just rule it out."

"I hope you're wrong for my wife's sake. He always makes her laugh."

"Probably nothing to it, Peel. But I have to see."

Jim nodded in agreement.

"I need you to be acting sheriff until I get back, if you will," Tilman went on. "I don't want to leave with no one in charge. Between the robberies and this Mulrooney fellow, I think too much is going on around here to just ride off for a few days. We should be back in a week at the most."

"I can handle it. Marie will like visiting Prosper for a day or two, and I have some business I can take care of here while I'm around."

The men shook hands, and Tilman watched Peel as he left. He was a good man and would have made a good sheriff if folks looked for ability first and political ties second.

"Marie?"

"In here, Jim." Marie Fleur looked up from a plush deep

green velvet chair, one of Prosper's recent acquisitions from New Orleans. "This chair is so comfortable, I'm falling asleep. I hoped you'd get home early enough so we could have lunch at the hotel."

She stood, and Peel again realized what a beautiful woman he had married. "Let me get your shawl, and we'll go. It is getting cool out there. Where is Prosper?" Jim had ordered the groom to hitch up and bring around the runabout, and they continued the conversation as they went out the front door.

"Oh, he's taking care of some business. I think it will be just the two of us." Marie Fleur smiled at her husband. Once again she wished she could be the woman he thought he had married. "Is that all right?"

"Marie! I think you're fishing for a compliment." Jim helped her into the little buggy. "You know having you all to myself is good for me. Besides"—he climbed onto the seat next to her—"for the next few days you will be the wife of the Chaffee County sheriff."

"What?" Marie stopped.

"Wagner is going to Tin Cup for a few days, and I'm filling in for him." Jim tapped the reins, and they started for town.

"Tin Cup? Where is Tin Cup?" Marie tried to keep the concern from her voice.

"It's west of here across Cottonwood Pass. Tin Cup's a mining camp, and rough. It's outside his jurisdiction, so he and Pegram will just be looking for answers to some questions they have. You know, like when somebody tells me somebody else stole his mule, and then I have to go find out what really happened."

Marie said nothing. She didn't like it when Jim talked to her as if she were a child who didn't understand what a lawman did.

"That's what they're doing." Jim chose his words carefully so that Marie would not guess that Wagner was investigating Marcel's gambling. He didn't want her to worry. "Wagner heard that a fellow in Buena Vista had a money scrape up there, and that seems to be reaching over into this neck of the woods."

Marie said nothing as they neared the hotel. She could tell

when Jim was holding back and not telling her something. She realized that she needed to talk to Marcel as soon as possible. Gambling, money scrapes, and Marcel went hand in hand, and if Tilman was headed for Tin Cup, then she had a nagging suspicion that somehow it involved Marcel. She leaned against her husband, trying to ignore the feeling of betrayal, the certainty that he hadn't told her the whole story.

Chapter Twenty-one

Marie Fleur liked to sleep late, and, as always, Jim got out of bed quietly so he didn't disturb her when he dressed and prepared to leave. He intended to be in the sheriff's office as soon as it was light. "Marie?" There was no answer, so Jim took a moment to watch her sleep, once more realizing how close his drinking had brought him to losing not only his self-respect, but also his wife. He eased the bedroom door shut behind him and went down to get breakfast before going to work. Prosper was reading the paper when Jim entered. A pot of coffee and a cloth-covered plate of biscuits were on the sideboard.

"You hungry, Jim?" Prosper spoke without looking up from his paper. "Charlene made some fresh biscuits that are still warm. Mighty good."

"Mornin', Prosper. Charlene, how about some bacon and eggs?" Jim buttered a biscuit, popped the whole thing into his mouth, and got a delicate china cup and saucer—no ordinary coffee mugs here—and poured steaming coffee. The small cup handle was impossible for a man's finger to fit into. Jim held the cup between thumb and forefinger, his little finger rising because there was no other place to put it. Still chewing, he settled into a chair across from Prosper and swallowed audibly. He poured coffee into his saucer, lifted it, and blew on it to cool it. Satisfied, he slurped the liquid from the saucer.

With obvious disapproval Prosper noted his son-in-law's manners but said nothing.

"If I stayed here all the time, I'd be as broad as I am tall." Jim reached behind him for a second biscuit as Charlene brought in a fresh pot of coffee.

After he finished breakfast, Jim tossed aside his napkin and took up a familiar banter with the cook. "Are you sure you don't want to come to Granite and take care of me and the missus?"

"Humph!" the woman grunted in pleasure. "How would Mr. Prosper manage?"

"What about me? Heaven knows Marie Fleur may be beautiful, but she still needs help when it comes to the kitchen. I haven't had eggs that good in a long time." He paused. "In fact, I think it was the last time we were here."

"Off you go, Mr. Peel." Laughter followed Peel as he left the room.

Marie Fleur didn't get downstairs until close to noon. After a skimpy breakfast in her room, she had waited until everyone was gone. She walked over to the hotel after stopping to look in the dry-goods store to pick up a piece of material she had ordered during her last visit. Marcel was waiting in the lobby just as she had instructed in the note she'd sent the day before. He contrived a look of surprise when he saw her, fully aware that every man in a room always turned to look when Marie Fleur entered.

"My favorite cousin. How nice to see you. You look beautiful as usual. Do you have time for tea?"

For the gossips looking and listening, Marie Fleur played her role well—the spoiled daughter of a rich man—and Marcel guided her to a seat by the window so they could see and be seen. Cousins meeting, the lovely Marie Fleur beaming smiles and handsome Marcel a gentleman in dress and manner, might arouse envy but certainly no suspicion. They had spoken to several acquaintances while waiting for their tea to arrive. When the waitress delivered the steaming pot, Marie Fleur poured as Marcel came to the heart of the matter. "Why the note? What is so urgent, and why is your wonderful husband filling in for our illustrious sheriff?"

"That's what I need to tell you. Jim is here because Tilman Wagner and Butter Pegram are on their way to Tin Cup."

"Why would they go there?"

"Jim said they were checking on somebody's money problems. He didn't say anything about you, but I know my husband pretty well." Marie Fleur studied Marcel, who avoided her eyes and stirred his tea. He played with the spoon, clearly uneasy with the news. "What aren't you telling me, Marcel? Did you leave acquaintances there who might know more than they should?"

Marcel frowned. "I had a woman I spent time with there. She wanted more than I had to give." He patted Marie Fleur's hand. "Don't worry. She's a nobody. I will make arrangements to see that their effort is wasted. That's all. You don't have to worry. There is nothing to implicate us here, though I am glad you let me know, so I can clear everything up."

The two finished their tea, and conversation waned, Marcel apprehensive and preoccupied. What if Sheriff Wagner found Sally? No one but Sally knew what he'd done. Would she tell? She didn't know about his and Marie Fleur's robberies. Just the fact that he'd helped himself get out of trouble there, and, really, it wasn't even a real bank, just a place in a general store where miners' money could be locked in a small safe. There had been barely enough money to pay off his debts.

Marcel was lucky that the store clerk never got a good look at his face. He was lucky, too, that he pulled the job the night before the town marshal was shot the moment he sat down to eat breakfast in a restaurant. Marcel quickly let slip in a couple of the saloons that there might be a link between the robbery and the shooting. The mere suggestion was enough to lead people to tie the robbery to the shooting. Angry citizens ran out and lynched the assassin, and everybody felt they had solved two crimes, so they forgot about it.

But Sally knew what he'd done. She was, once, a good-looking woman—exclusively his woman, for she thought they'd marry one day—and now he'd have to shut her up. His recollections were interrupted when Marie Fleur stood, so he rose as well, got her chair, and bowed slightly at the waist. Polite yet cool, she excused herself.

On a whim she considered riding out to the site of her papa's new house, or Prosper's Pride, as she had heard it called behind his back. Why he thought he needed such a large house mystified her. There would be no children to fill the rooms. She was the last in the line. What was he doing? Every time Marie Fleur brought up the subject, her father shifted the conversation to something different.

Perhaps in time she could get used to the house. If he only knew how much tales about the half-built shell tore at her, he would surely have it razed. But how could she tell him? Her father's lies still stung. Once they had been close, but now she felt a gulf developing between them. How could she trust him enough to admit her failure?

Chapter Twenty-two

If Marie Fleur had acted on her impulse and gone to the half-built shell of her father's house, she would have seen Marcel nervously pacing what would become the dining room while he waited for Lester Smith to join him. He and Lester had done business before. Marcel didn't care for the man, but he knew that he could be bought cheaply. After all, Smith, or whatever his real name was, had been helpful in the past. Marcel looked out the high, narrow windows, each close to seven feet tall. His uncle had such pretentious plans. Marcel admired the man's tenacity but couldn't help but feel resentment. What a waste of money. Marie Fleur would never live here. Prosper would likely never stay in the house. And the cost was enormous and growing with each year.

"You admiring the chandelier up there?" Lester stood in the doorway, smirking. He knew he'd come up on Marcel and caught him unaware. "Your uncle really dreams big, don't he?"

"Never mind, Smith. I need you to do some work for me. You think you could use some extra cash?"

"Man can never have too much money. What do you need, Marcel?" Lester sat down on a stack of lumber. He pulled a medicine bottle from his coat pocket and took a swallow. He smacked his lips and took another swig. "Mighty good." He held the bottle out to Marcel.

Marcel shook his head. "Sheriff Wagner and Deputy Pegram are on their way to Tin Cup. Apparently they don't have enough to do here in Buena Vista, so they're going to snoop around there. Folks there know too much about my gambling."

"So? That's no big problem, Marcel. Most people around

here know you gamble a bit too much. It ain't like it's illegal. No secret there."

"Yeah, but you remember Sally Meachum?" Marcel paused. "Little thing. Worked at the Silver Thread Saloon in Tin Cup?"

"Yeah. Weren't you two kinda close for a while?"

"For a time. Anyway, she thought it was more than it was, and she started saying some things that aren't right, and I don't want to hear any more rumors." Marcel straightened his collar and adjusted his cuff links. "I'm trying to stay on Uncle's good side, and I don't need any cheap saloon girl getting in my way. You get my point, Lester?"

"Surely do, Marcel. I'll be on my way this afternoon. I can outride Wagner and Pegram without any problem. It'll cost you, though. I don't like to rough up women."

"I'll pay."

The two men arrived at a price and parted ways, Lester heading on up the road to Cottonwood Pass. He'd stop partway up the pass and spend the night and be at Tin Cup soon enough.

Chapter Twenty-three

It was midmorning of a gray day. A sullen, drizzling rain was falling when Lester Smith slogged through ankle-deep mud and knocked on the door of a two-room log cabin. Lester had looked around for Wagner and Pegram but didn't see them in town, so he reckoned they were still on the trail. He knew that he had the upper hand, since he knew where Sally lived, but it would be best not to tarry.

"Come on in. I'm decent."

Lester smiled to himself as he tugged a rawhide strip that lifted the inside bar to open the door. Sally Meachum's cabin sat off by itself behind the row of saloons.

"Lester Smith. Take off that slicker, and hang it on a peg. And wipe your feet. What are you doing here?" Sally stood by a small wood-burning stove, her frilly robe providing little warmth on such a cold morning. "I'm freezing. Shut the door, and come on in." She tried to look nonchalant, but the scared look in her eyes told Lester all he needed to know.

He sat down. "Got any coffee, Sal?"

She poured him a mug and sat on a three-legged stool across from him at a table built onto the cabin wall. The early-morning light from the small window unkindly showed her to be a careworn woman old before her time. The life of a saloon girl was short, and if you didn't marry, you ended up cleaning floors and taking in wash, or worse, before you were thirty. Lester knew all about it, since his mother had been forced into the same life, and she had died when he was small, tuberculosis no discriminator about age.

"I'm here on account of Marcel, Sally."

"Yeah? How is he?" She leaned forward hopefully. "Does he want me to come to him?"

Lester didn't look at Sally. He knew what she was, and he also knew Marcel for the person he was. "Nah. In fact, he's a little upset, Sally girl. It seems like you let it be known that when Marcel was up here, he got into a scrape."

"But, Lester, he did, and he was the one throwing money around like there was lots more where that come from. Well, he did until his luck ran out and he lost it all. Then those men came after him. But he . . ."

Lester stood up and leaned over Sally, his eyes cold. "Listen, Sal, and listen good. Marcel don't want you saying anything else about any money or any scrape. Not to nobody. You got me? Some people might wonder how he got out of that little mess, and we don't want no extra look-sees comin' his way. Understand?"

"You know I'd never say anything to hurt him, Lester. He is too important to me. I—"

She paused, not sure what to say.

Lester patted her on the hand. "I know, Sally. Just keep your mouth shut, and anybody comes to ask around, just keep silent, and you'll do fine." Lester made to leave the room. "I'd hate for anything to happen to your old man. I know how important he is to you. He needs the money you bring in, that's for sure. That accident down at the mine last year stove up your pa bad, and he's lucky to have you to look after him."

"What are you saying, Lester?" Sally's shoulders sagged, her face looking resigned to another of the defeats that had become her life, her small hands clenched at her sides.

"Nothin', Sally. Nothin' at all." Lester flipped a silver dollar onto the table. "Thanks for the coffee." He donned his slicker and quietly closed the door and stepped out into the rain. Now for the rest of the job.

Chapter Twenty-four

Following a muddy freight road down the mountains from Cottonwood Pass, Tilman and Butter, gum ponchos shedding most of the steady rain that fell, at last descended below the bottoms of the clouds to see the valley below. The road ran close to Willow Creek, which entered the town from the north, the direction they'd follow to reach the pass on their return. The small mining camp of Tin Cup sat nestled in the valley just below ten thousand feet in elevation where Willow Creek, Bertha Gulch, and Slaughterhouse Gulch came together. Tin Cup was dominated in the east by a towering and rugged mountain that reached over thirteen thousand feet. It was a raw place, subject to the whims of whatever lawless element assumed gun authority. The last three town marshals had all been shot dead.

"I've been to some bad places, but I think Tin Cup might be one of the worst." Butter got down off his horse and looked at the town. Midmorning did little to brighten the layer of clouds covering the valley, adding to the grim air of tiredness that enfolded the town.

"This place has run through the silver and now seems to be on its way to being a ghost town." Tilman tied his horse to the hitching rail outside the hotel. There was no porch. They entered through the front door and found themselves in a dark hallway. To the left a small room contained a registration desk. There was no clerk in sight. "I rode here when I was hunting Dan's killer several years ago. It's changed."

The two ducked into the dining room on the opposite side of the hall. Only two other men were in the room, each alone at separate tables. Tilman wrinkled his nose at the smell of old grease and unwashed bodies hanging in the air like a fog. They made their way to a table by a flyspecked, dirty window, draping their dripping ponchos over a vacant chair.

A beanpole of a woman wheezed into the room from the kitchen, struggling for breath. She stood by the table, left fist on one hip, a tattered menu in the other hand. "What'll it be?" She suppressed a racking cough deep in her chest. She wore a rough cotton dress that was too big and hung on her like a sack.

Tilman and Butter ordered coffee.

"Be right up." From the kitchen came the sounds of more coughing.

Tilman shook his head. "Consumption?"

Butter nodded agreement. "These places are either getting worse, or I'm getting old." He looked around, thinking of Neala and her clean kitchen and his four young ones at home. "I miss my missus, and that's a fact."

The waitress brought the coffee. "Two bits."

Tilman lifted his right hand from the table, revealing a double eagle. "That's yours if you answer my questions."

Her eyes narrowed to slits as she cast a furtive glance around the room. "Depends on the questions."

"You been in Tin Cup long?"

"Coupla years." She drew a wheezing breath.

"You ever know a fellow who used to live around here, a real swell, a Frenchy?"

"Yeah. A gambler. Had a funny name, like 'DeRow' or some such." Her cheeks puffed with another suppressed cough.

Tilman leaned back in his chair, careful to reveal nothing. "That'd be the one."

"You the law?" After another cough, she wiped her mouth with the back of one hand.

"Chaffee County Sheriff."

"No skin off my back. My name's Opal." The woman's hungry eyes were fixed on the gold piece. "He left town six or eight months back. About the time the last marshal got shot. You gonna gimme that money?"

"One more question. Is there anybody still in town might know about him?"

Opal smiled. "Tim Meachum's daughter was his gal."

"Where can we find her?"

"Tim got hurt in the mines. Ain't seen Sally in ages. Maybe she left town."

"I don't really want any coffee." Tilman pushed the coin across the table.

A clawlike hand scooped up the coin, and the woman was gone.

"Let's get out of here."

The rain had stopped. Standing by their horses, Tilman looked at Butter. "She's lying."

"What part?"

"She told us just enough to earn the money and no more."

"Hey you, Sheriff." Opal appeared in the alley between the buildings, beckoning for Tilman to follow.

"What do you suppose she wants?" Butter asked Tilman as they made their way around the building.

"I don't know, Butter. Maybe she thought of something."

"You boys get a move on. I can't stay out here long, or they'll come looking for me." The woman coughed, nervously glancing around to see that they weren't being followed. "As you can see, my looks ain't what they used to be, so I do some waitressin' but mostly the cleaning and laundry for the hotel." She held out a callous hand with cracked, broken nails. "How much you willin' to pay for information about Sally Meachum and that man who done her wrong?" A gap showed where one of her front teeth used to be. Her face was marred with several scars, some still red and not completely healed.

Butter protested. "Hey, the sheriff—"

Tilman held up a hand to shush Butter. He couldn't determine Opal's age. It could have been anything between twenty and forty. Life had been hard on her, and time had not treated her kindly. "There might be more. Depends on what you know, Opal. We're from down around Buena Vista, and I need to know about a man named Marcel Devereaux." Tilman paused.

"If Meachum's daughter was his gal, I want to talk to her. Do you know where she is?"

"Opal!" A shouted call came from inside the saloon. "Get back in here!"

"I've got to go. My place is that one back behind the hotel." Opal pointed down the alley to a shanty that looked more like a shed than anything else. The door stood at a tilt, and Tilman could not imagine a woman spending a winter in a place like that. "Meet me there after I finish cleaning up the dinner dishes, and I'll tell you a thing or two. I want money to get to Denver. I got folks there who'll take me in. I'd just as soon work for them as work up here. Will you help me or not?" She looked over Tilman, clearly afraid to count on these men.

"We'll meet you, Opal, and we'll have the money. You help us, and we'll help you get out." Tilman felt for this poor woman and thought he saw a faint glimmer of hope in her dead eyes.

"Deal?"

She nodded and turned and hurried back inside the hotel.

"Makes you realize the world ain't always a good place, is it?" Butter turned to Tilman. "You think she knows anything?"

"Doesn't much matter. Opal has paid her dues. Time she gets out while she still can."

"County pays?"

"Sure does."

The two men rode out beyond the town and found one of several cemeteries bordered by piles of mine spoil. "I heard that this town can't keep an honest lawman. Old Andy Jamison was a man I knew, and he came up here in eighty-three and met with a little 'incident,' you might say," Butter mused aloud. "The two after him, Rivers and Frank Emerson, only lasted a few months. Emerson went under about the same time Marcel came to Buena Vista. You play the game the outlaws' way, or you don't play."

The two men waited till Opal got off work.

Chapter Twenty-five

I don't know a lot, but Sally—she's Tim Meachum's daughter—and Marcel Dev'ro ate at the hotel when he was here, and one night they had words. I overheard him telling her that he owed a man in the Slaughterhouse a big debt. He said he had a way to take care of it, though. She was crying." Opal looked at Tilman and Butter as they sat in her small home drinking tea poured from a cracked pot. "Sal ain't a bad girl. She has an old man who got hurt in the mines, and she takes care of him the best she can. Guess she thought Marcel was the answer to her prayers." Opal snorted, plainly torn between liking Sally and thinking she was being used. One more fit of coughing caught her, and this time Tilman noted the telltale red spots on her handkerchief. "Anyway, she works at the Silver Crest Saloon and lives in one of the shacks in back. Won't be hard to find."

Tilman stood, handing Opal a drawstring sack, which she quickly opened. She looked inside and said, "Hey, Sheriff, there's too much in here. What else do you—"

"Opal, you get out of here while you can. Go and find your people. Thanks for your help."

"Ma'am." Butter touched his hat, and they headed out into the late afternoon, hoping to catch Sally Meachum before she went to work.

"I don't know nothing, mister." Sally Meachum was small, mousy, and obviously frightened. She stood at her door, holding it closed as she looked through a crack. "I haven't seen Marcel since he run out on me. I have to go, or I'll be late for work."

94

The darkly weathered wooden door closed with a thump. "Don't reckon the little lady wanted to chat." Butter smiled as he and Tilman turned to leave. "Do you want to follow her over to the saloon and see what we can find out?"

"Don't see much point, Butter. Somebody must have put the scare on her. I think we're done here. Let's have a drink at the Silver Crest and, unless you have any objection, I think I'll spend the night at the livery. A pile of hay's better'n that hotel."

Several hours and a couple of drinks later, Tilman and Butter had witnessed two fistfights, one man drawing a gun on another over a saloon girl, and Sally Meachum trying to stay far away from them on the opposite side of the room. "You ready, Pegram?"

"I was ready when we got here. Let's get some sleep and head for home in the morning."

Chapter Twenty-six

"Old Dish Face here is the worst I ever saw to fill his lights and stick out his belly when you saddle him." Leading his horse through the door of Barton's Stables into the cold, early-morning light, Butter dabbed the reins over a hitching post and then kneed his mount. The horse sucked up his gut, and Butter quickly tightened the saddle girth. "If I don't catch him now, me and him'll part company when we start up Cotton-wood Pass." Finished, he jammed his gloved hands deep into the pockets of his long coat. He exhaled, watching the condensation of his breath fly away. "That north wind cuts right through you!" Both the condensation and the sound of his voice whipped away on the rushing wind so that he had to shout to be heard.

Tilman swung into his saddle, and Butter handed up the lead for the packhorse.

Tilman's eyes watered in the cold. He knuckled his eyes to clear them. "Won't be so bad once we get out of this valley and into the trees." His mount was eager for the trail, and so was Tilman.

Settling himself into the saddle, Butter drew up alongside Tilman, and they set out on the long freight road they would follow back across the mountains to Cottonwood Pass and down to Buena Vista, just over twenty miles of travel altogether. After the road crossed the pass, it was all downhill.

As they passed the last of the miners' shanties at the edge of town, Tilman watched in amazement as Butter dug into an inside pocket of his coat and withdrew a biscuit. They'd ridden less than half a mile and finished breakfast hardly an hour earlier. Butter bit into the biscuit with relish.

"Say, old man, was there ever a time when you got enough to eat?"

Butter took another bite and mumbled around the mouthful of bread. "Eat when you can, I always say. A man never knows when he'll get a chance for more."

Tilman shivered and turned up the collar on his waxed light brown canvas coat to keep the wind off his neck. His coat was new and had a warm blanket-wool lining. It was a gift from Catherine—she said a sheriff couldn't wear an old, patched, and stained work jacket—and he was grateful for her thoughtfulness. Talk died away as both men settled onto the trail. Thoughts wandered. Tilman tried to make sense of what he'd learned in Tin Cup, while Butter remembered a likely place he'd seen on the way up where they could stop for dinner and to rest the horses at noon. It offered shelter and a fast-moving stream of sweet water, near which he planned to build a fire to make coffee.

Their vigilance waned in the cold as they rode into the morning. A train of six freight wagons bound for Tin Cup provided welcome diversion and elicited Butter's speculation as to what manner of edibles lay hidden under the canvas covers on the wagon boxes, but Tilman could not be drawn into Butter's talk. Butter gave up.

The dinner break refreshed them, but by the middle of the afternoon, as they made their way down from Cottonwood Pass toward Buena Vista, the conversation sparked by food and hot coffee ebbed, then stopped, and dullness returned. The road was rough, with ruts in the low places. They let their horses have their heads to find the best footing.

"Not much traffic around here," Butter commented.

Tilman nodded, his mind trying to work out if Sally Meachum could possibly have had anything to add or was really just a silly young woman who fell for men who appeared wild and mysterious. Hard to tell. "You think we should have worried that Meachum gal more? Asked a few more questions?"

"No, Tilman. Wasn't much use I could see. Whatever she once was, she reminds me of a whupped puppy. I reckon she told us what she knew." Butter ambled behind Tilman. "And I don't think that was much. Hardly worth the trip, to my mind."

Tilman nodded agreement, and the two men went along the rough road, their attention taken with the task of getting home. Both men knew better than to relax their vigilance completely. Complacency had been the cause of many a good man going under the sod too soon. Still, they didn't expect to find trouble. And because they didn't, it nearly cost them their lives.

They approached a narrow gap through the steep-sided hills, a gap cut by a prehistoric Cottonwood Creek in wetter times, when the melting of mountain glaciers sent massive amounts of water coursing toward the valley below. The road passed closely between massive granite boulders. They rode single file with Tilman in the lead. Butter watched a mule deer off to the left grazing in a clump of aspen raise his head, looking not at the riders but ahead of them. Too late, he realized that was wrong.

Tilman's horse jerked its head up, wild eyes rolling white, then stumbled as the sound of a gunshot boomed from the rocks. The animal fell, spilling its rider into the road, splotches of blood showing dark on Tilman's coat. Butter's spurs raked his horse, and he reined hard right into the brush along the road, fumbling for the rifle in his saddle scabbard. He heard another shot, sawed back on the reins, and stepped to the ground as his horse spun. He took cover behind the massive trunk of a ponderosa pine as his horse ambled off and stood waiting nearby.

"Tilman? Are you okay?" Butter could see the soles of Tilman's boots.

Tilman lay sprawled in the road, stunned by the fall. He heard his horse's last long sigh as its life breath escaped. He opened his eyes and looked at the notch in the rocks where he'd seen gun smoke when the shot was fired. A man there held a rifle at the ready but was craning his neck, looking for Butter's hiding place. The man ignored Tilman, confident he no longer posed a threat. As Tilman watched, his anger flared. *Stupid! I let myself fall into a trap like a greenhorn idiot.*

Suddenly the man moved to get a better angle on Butter, crabbing backward into the rocks. Tilman stretched out an arm to his horse, pulled his rifle from the saddle, and crawled into the brush, being careful to do it quietly. His hot anger gave way to a dangerously cold and deadly determination. Adrenaline sang in his blood, and an old, familiar feeling came over him, a calm certainty that he was better at this game than most men and that the other would soon fall under his gun. *I can take this one,* he thought. Time stood still, and Tilman reverted to the man he used to be years before.

Butter's senses, sharpened by the danger of imminent death, took in everything yet told him nothing. Silence but for the wind moaning through the pines. Only the treetops moved, swaying, pushed by that same wind that served to muffle any sound a man might make as he changed position for a better shot. Back up the trail over which they had come, the packhorse stood in the middle of the road, head down, waiting. Tilman's horse lay where it had fallen, dead.

Cautiously Butter knelt, risked a quick look around the tree trunk, and drew back. Not a sign of anyone moving. Where was Tilman? Hadn't he been killed? Butter had seen his friend fall and had seen the blood on him. But now, where could Tilman have gotten to? Had the shooter dragged the body off the road into the bushes? Or was he not dead after all? Had Tilman crawled off under his own power?

A pebble hit his sleeve. It had to be Tilman! That's how he announced his presence when he couldn't risk a sound. Where could he be? *There!* Butter saw him in the brush across the road.

Tilman crouched, his eyes glittering as brightly as a stalking wolf's, white showing around pale irises, thin-lipped mouth set in a grim line. A thrill of fear caught in Butter's chest, for there was a frightening hardness in Tilman's eyes Butter had not seen in years. There was indeed blood on his coat, but he appeared to be moving about all right. If he was hit, it must not be bad. Tilman held up one finger and then pointed to the rocks directly in front of Butter. Butter nodded. *One bushwhacker, and he's on this side of the road.*

Tilman motioned to his left. Butter understood that Tilman intended to slip around to find a clear shot at the bushwhacker from behind. Butter would have to divert the shooter's attention. Raising his rifle, he fired three shots as quickly as he could work the action. "Who are you?" he called out.

Silence.

"Can we make a deal?"

Silence.

Butter looked around the tree and through the underbrush saw Tilman rise, step into the open road, and take aim with his rifle, shouting, "Make a move, and I'll kill you!" Then Tilman fired, worked the lever on his rifle, and fired again. He brought his rifle to waist level and chambered a fresh round. "I got him."

"Was there just the one?"

"Looks like it. There's only one horse tied back here."

Butter followed the road through the gap and into the rocks. He could see Tilman kneeling beside the body of the bushwhacker. With a shock, Butter suddenly saw the head and shoulders of another man rise above a rock no more than thirty feet away. The man raised a pistol and fired on Tilman, then thumbed back the hammer and fired a second shot. He missed both times.

"Look out!" Butter shouted uselessly as he spun and fired from the hip. His round struck the rock in front of the shooter and ricocheted upward, striking the man under his chin, snapping his head back, and sending his hat flying. The pistol fell from his hand, and the man slumped out of sight behind the rock.

Butter, holding his rifle at the ready, edged over to the rock to see if the man was dead or alive. A quick look revealed that the man would never again be a threat to anyone. Butter sniffed. "Hey, I found a empty whiskey bottle back here." He turned to Tilman. "This fool was stinkin' drunk! It's a wonder he could even stand up on his own."

Tilman shook his head. "Old man, you and me should be horse-whipped. We weren't paying attention, and then, when we got bushwhacked, we figured there was only one man sent to take care of both of us." Tilman put a hand on Butter's shoulder. "You saved my bacon. Thanks."

"How about we not make a habit of this?" Butter went to check the pockets of the man he'd shot. He found nothing.

They studied the scene before them. The first shooter had piled smaller rocks to form a parapet between larger rocks. He'd spread a blanket on the ground to lie on while he waited. "You know that feller?"

Tilman searched the man's pockets but found nothing to indicate who he was or where he came from. "Never saw him before. You?"

"No, but it looks to me like he was expecting somebody. Or us. How'd he know we'd be coming along here?"

"Beats me. Look at this." He tossed a tobacco sack to Butter. "Double eagles! Ten of 'em."

Tilman stood and looked down at the body. "Either he got a hundred dollars in advance for you and a hundred for me, or maybe it was half now and the rest when we were done for."

"That's likely so. I think it's safe to say that this one's the hired killer. He must've tried to go on the cheap and hire that bar-sweep over there to side him."

"To save a few dollars, he ended up paying a much higher price."

Butter scratched his chin. "Who wants us dead?"

"I can think of several names." Tilman folded the man's blanket around the body and covered the face.

Butter saw the grim set of Tilman's mouth. It was a look he'd not seen in a long time. *Killing's not done yet,* he thought. *Somebody's gonna pay.* "Maybe we ought to bury these two."

"If we leave 'em," Tilman said as he dug fresh cartridges from a pocket and shoved them into the loading port of his rifle, "it'll be a warning to whoever hired 'em and to others like him. The price for trying to kill a lawman just went up. Way up."

Butter stepped in front of Tilman, his face inches from his friend's. "Lemme tell you something. I'm not going along with that. When we get back to Buena Vista, I'm gonna send the undertaker up here to get these two. If the county won't pay,

I'll take from that sack of blood money and pay the undertaker myself. If the county's too cheap to bury 'em, I'll do it and give what's left to the church's Widows and Orphans Fund before I'll let the county see a penny of it."

Eyes unblinking, the two glared in silence.

"It's inhuman to leave 'em out here for the buzzards."

"They tried to kill us."

"That's right, Tilman. But you're an honorable man. That's why you're sheriff of our little county. Because you have rules, and you live by them, and people know that your word is good. Go back to being a man set on vengeance and getting even, and you lose more than the day-to-day battle. You lose your soul."

Tilman finally nodded. "You're right. No need for us to stoop to their level."

Butter shifted his feet, the confrontation ended. He'd made his point. "I'll get this'un's horse. We'll drag your'n off the road and strip off your saddle. I'll find that other feller's mount."

"Yeah. Let's get going." The fury was gone from Tilman. "Hey, Butter?"

"Yeah?"

"The county'll pay."

Chapter Twenty-seven

The sweeper went around extinguishing lanterns in the bar as morning sunlight brightened the streets outside the Delaware Hotel. The sleepy bartender rested his elbows on the bar, yawned, and watched as most of the remaining players in the poker game folded. He was bored. The waitress stood by the end of the bar. Without taking his eyes off the game, he spoke to her. "That Frenchy doing any better?"

"Nah, and he's in pretty deep," she answered.

Marcel and a blue-eyed, blond-haired Swedish woman gambler from San Francisco were the only players left. She'd demurely introduced herself as Mrs. Mortensen, a miner's wife. In reality she'd been hired to play for the house, and she was expert in handling cards. Being full-figured and knowing in the ways of men, she traveled with a steamer truck holding a collection of off-the-shoulder gowns, all intended to distract a man's attention.

Marcel had fallen for her charms and given no thought to the possibility that the house had chosen to hire a woman like her. He spread his cards with a flourish. "Full house, kings over tens."

His opponent expertly fanned her cards on the velvet playing surface. "Four aces!" She raked the money from the table into a drawstring purse and smiled coyly. "And I think I'll call it a night or, should I say, morning?"

Across the room the bartender motioned to the waitress. "It's over. Go get the boss."

In a desperate ploy to recover his losses, Marcel tried to charm the lady into another hand. "You're the best I've ever seen! Not only are you beautiful but a master card player as

103

well!" He stood in deference to the lady. "Please teach me how you do that."

But a winning smile from a handsome young man held no allure for her. "Nice try, kid." With a throaty laugh she left him alone at the table.

A clean-shaven man wearing an expensively tailored suit slid into her vacant seat across from Marcel. The man smelled of the peppermint oil he dosed his sore throat with—a tablespoonful three times a day every day. He spoke with a gravelly voice, the lasting result of a hard punch that had nearly crushed his Adam's apple in a Natchez riverboat saloon some years back. *"Ahem."* He cleared his throat. "Devereaux, you owe the house . . ." He pulled a tally book from his vest pocket, thumbed the pages, and paused to clear his voice. "Let me see . . ." He paused again, then continued. "Since you got here three days ago, you've lost a little over nineteen thousand dollars and run up a bar tab of another thousand."

Marcel poured the dregs from a Champagne bottle into a crystal flute and upended the bottle in the ice bucket. He sipped nonchalantly. "I'm good for it."

"I got instructions. You gotta pay up, one week from today. The boys upstairs won't wait like last time."

"That was unfortunate. It won't happen again. Like I said, tell them I'm good for it."

Later, at the Leadville railroad station, his hands began shaking when abject fear took hold of him. He owed a massive amount of money to hard men who lived in the shadows, men who'd kill him as easily as someone swatting a mosquito. Fear made him physically ill. Marcel used a fine silk handkerchief to wipe his mouth after nervously retching in the men's washroom. When his train was called, he boarded the Valley shuttle to return to Buena Vista.

He found his seat in a chair car. It was filthy, with newspapers scattered on the floor, spittoons overflowing, and cigarette and cigar butts littering the aisle. He tossed his Gladstone bag into the overhead luggage rack and collapsed into the seat. What could he do? Beg his uncle for forgiveness and more money to settle his debts? No, he'd already tested Prosper's patience. He needed a lot of money, desperately. His cut from the robberies was long gone.

What to do? Marie Fleur always wanted things to be tidy. That was good, but it didn't pay as fast or as much as he needed. He had to get enough cash to leave Colorado and go back to New Orleans, or maybe San Antonio, Texas. He'd heard there was a good bit of money to be had there, and that might give him a whole new start. No one would know him, and he could begin all over. He stared out the car window at a landscape ravaged by years of mining and virtually denuded of trees by logging operations undertaken carelessly to supply shoring timber for the mines. Colorado was great if you had money and power, but it could also be a very dangerous place.

By the time the train pulled into the Buena Vista station, Marcel felt hopeless, for there seemed to be no answer to his problem. Skip town? What choices did he have? Where could he go? How would he support himself? He'd lost his ready cash. When he stepped onto the platform, the first thing he saw on the other side of the platform was stacks of silver ingots waiting to be loaded onto the D&RG train for the Denver Mint. The three men standing idle by the bars were not even armed! *Somebody's getting rich,* he thought. He looked away, one hand going to his pocket in search of loose change, thinking about stopping for a drink before confronting Uncle Prosper. He halted on the platform, and his face broke into a smile. He looked again at the ingots. He'd found an answer for his problem!

Chapter Twenty-eight

Rob a train?" Marie Fleur's eyes widened. "Tell me you're not serious, *chéri*."

Marcel expected exactly this reaction from his cousin, the very reason he had come to visit her at her home in Granite while Jim was at work. "Of course I am."

"But how can we stop a train? What about all the people on it? When we go into a bank, there are only a few people, and they are easy to control." She paced in front of the window of her small parlor, her agitation demanding expression in movement—four steps, turn, four steps, turn—and her words came almost without pause. "The stagecoaches were easy because there were few people there as well. Have you lost your mind?"

"Others have robbed trains. Remember the James Gang? They were successful. I've given this much thought. I know how to stop the train. We must stop the train in a cut—even better if we choose one where the track curves—and then we have only to deal with the clerk in the express car. . . ."

Marie Fleur held up her hands to interrupt her cousin. "Jesse James was shot dead several years ago."

Marcel was wearing her down. "Yes, but not while robbing a train!"

"But what if there is more than one clerk?"

"Never mind. We'll deal with them just as we deal with the driver and express guard on a stagecoach." Marcel left his chair and stepped in front of her, taking her arms in his hands to steady her. "Think of it! When the cash exchange for the silver and gold shipments returns to this Valley from the mint in Denver, there are not tens of thousands of dollars, but hundreds of thousands! *Hundreds!* With one robbery alone we could be set for life. We could go away from here and live grandly forever!"

His enthusiasm proved contagious. Marie Fleur thought of the beauty of New Orleans and the gracious society there. The seed of an idea Marcel had planted appealed to his cousin's sense of daring, and her eyes took on a faraway look as the seed germinated. Marie Fleur imagined a place far from windy, cold, dirty Granite with its half a dozen trains whistling and rumbling past the front of her home every day. She thought of her complexion and how she struggled against chapping and redness. The dresses she could buy with all that money . . .

"No, it's too dangerous." She shrugged, giving voice to her doubts. "Too much can go wrong. People could get hurt."

"Not if we're careful. If we plan and don't take unnecessary chances, what could go wrong?"

Marie Fleur paced. She pictured. She planned. She turned, clapping her hands in anticipation. "Nothing, if we're careful." She studied her cousin's face. "Or everything. But life is short, is it not? Well," Marie Fleur said, and she began to smile, "maybe you're right after all."

"You agree?"

"Why don't we open that Champagne you brought and drink a toast to . . ."

"To what?"

Her smile became an impish grin. "To money, *chéri.*"

Marcel laughed while pouring the wine. He was secretly relieved that she had been so easily convinced to go along with his plan. He had expected resistance, maybe even hysterics from his pampered cousin. To think! He'd soon have the means to pay off the people in Leadville, and Uncle need never know any of it. Once again he'd be welcomed at the tables.

The Champagne bubbles tickled Marie Fleur's nose. *Why just one train?* she thought. If one brought them riches, another would bring fabulous riches. After all, one could never have too much money, could one?

Chapter Twenty-nine

Two miles south of Granite, where the railroad bed was cut into the mountainside a few yards from the Arkansas River, they waited atop an embankment overlooking the curving railroad tracks fifteen feet below. Marie Fleur's mare danced nervously at the sound of the locomotive's shrill whistle echoing off the mountain behind them. The excitement was almost more than she could bear. She stole a glance at Marcel, who sat his horse beside her.

"Soon it will be here." He was as calm as if he were sitting in her parlor, sipping *café au lait*. "Your bandanna, *chérie*."

Marie Fleur tugged her hat brim down low, then lifted her bandanna to cover the rest of her face but for her eyes. She looked like Marcel and the other two men, only shapeless figures under their long dusters, unrecognizable behind their masks. Her long hair was in a tight bun under her hat, and she wore no makeup, and she had even taken to using a little dirt on her face to make it look more lined. With a thrill she saw black smoke above the trees, heard the rhythmic chuffing of the engine drawing closer. The moment was near!

Marcel drew his pistol, and with his right elbow bent he held the gun muzzle up and ready. With a fleeting thought he saw in his mind's eye the striking figure he must present. The others raised their guns as he did. All that remained was to wait.

Cooter and Lars Swenson now rode with Marcel and Marie Fleur. Since the stagecoach robbery the two seemed to follow orders well and made no trouble. One of the reasons Marcel had recruited them was that they had no ties to anyone but each other. They were brothers, separated by a year, and had each done time in the local jail for petty crimes. Neither of them made much of a criminal, but they followed orders and didn't mind taking the risks. Plus, Cooter claimed to know a little about dynamiting, and Marie Fleur thought that might eventually come in handy.

When the three men and Marie Fleur were in their tan dusters with bandannas up and hats pulled low, they were indistinguishable from one another. And that was a good thing. No one stood out, so no one was at risk. Cooter and Lars also kept their mouths shut. Neither of them talked unless they had to. Truth be told, when they were young, their pa had beat them more often than not for talking too much or talking back, so they had long gotten out of the habit of conversing with others.

In the railroad cut below them two heavy wooden cross ties lay across the rails. Marcel was certain his plan would work, and they would derail the locomotive before the engineer could bring the rushing train to a halt. He had told the others that the cut would contain the derailing cars, and certainly no one would be injured. They would force the express car door open and make off with the contents of the safe. Surely the whole thing would take less than ten minutes.

"There she comes!"

The locomotive rounded the curve and entered the cut. They saw the engineer's face in the cab window, his right elbow resting on the sill. They saw the precise moment when the engineer noticed the ties on the track ahead—his head leaned farther out and then disappeared back inside the cab. Suddenly the whistle screamed repeatedly, white steam spurting into the cool morning sunlight, but the train was not slowing down.

The four inexperienced train robbers were amazed to see the cowcatcher at the locomotive's front smash into the ties, scooping them up and sending them flying end over end off the tracks as effortlessly as a child playing pick-up sticks. The train thundered past, iron wheels clacking on the rail joints, while Marie Fleur glimpsed unconcerned faces of passengers framed in the rail cars' windows. Incredibly, one passenger saw the riders, had no idea of their intent, and gave a friendly wave of the hand.

Marie Fleur turned to Marcel, who sat motionless, staring at the passing train. "Don't they know they're supposed to stop?"

Like water flowing around a bridge, smoke and cinders from the engine's funnel washed around the horsemen. Marie Fleur squinted as the acrid coal smoke burned her eyes, and she began coughing, but the smoke quickly dissipated.

As if awakening from a trance, Marcel shouted an oath and fired his pistol in the direction of the caboose quickly receding down the tracks toward Buena Vista. A man dressed in oil-stained bib overalls stood on the rear platform of the caboose, and when he heard the shots, he ducked back inside.

This was all wrong! Marcel inwardly fumed. It was not how he had planned it.

Marie Fleur jerked the bandanna from her face. "Lars, you and Cooter go and keep out of sight until I send for you. Go now!" The men wheeled their horses down the slope, crossed the tracks, and passed from sight into the thick growth of piñon and aspen trees. Brutally she hauled her reins, pulling her mount alongside Marcel's so that she was face-to-face with her cousin. "You know how to stop a train, you said. Pah! You know nothing!"

Marcel was speechless.

Marie Fleur's eyes flashed with cold anger. "Now I understand why Aunt Blanche sent you to my father. You are a weak man, cousin. You talk, but talk is empty. Next time *I* make the plan for the train. Next time *I* choose the time and the place. Next time *I* am the one who gives the orders!"

"You can't speak to me like that! I won't stand for it."

"Ah, but you will. You are afraid my father will learn how your face became bruised and why."

"You wouldn't dare . . ."

"Don't be too sure, *chéri.*" She spurred her horse, calling over her shoulder, "Wait for me to contact you."

A short time later the telegrapher's delivery boy ran into Tilman's office. "They tried to rob the train!"

Tilman dropped the sheaf of wanted posters he'd been reading. "What?"

"Come to the station quick. The engineer says somebody tried to stop the train just outside of Granite." The boy milked every moment of his dramatic importance. "And when the train didn't stop, they shot at the brakeman!"

Tilman shouldered into his coat and hooked his hat from the rack. "Do you know if anybody got hurt?"

"No, sir, I don't think so."

"Let's go see."

At the station a small crowd gathered to hear the engineer, still perched in the cab of his idling engine, answering questions shouted up from the crowd. Tilman called the man down and steered him into the stationmaster's office, where he hoped to get the story straight. The conductor waved his watch, protesting loudly, "What about our schedule? We're behind already!"

The stationmaster scribbled a note and passed it to his telegrapher. "Get this to the home office right now. They'd better hear the news from us before it gets out."

The telegrapher's fist began tapping out code. Things were moving fast, and Tilman was glad when Butter pushed his way through the murmuring crowd to join him and the engineer. He needed a friendly face.

"What's all this excitement?"

"Well, old man, looks like we've got a botched train robbery on our hands."

A reporter from the *Leadville Chronicle* stuck his head and shoulders through the office window. "Hey, Sheriff. We can get this on the front page in an extra edition. Was it the Flower Gang?"

Tilman leaned down so that only Butter could hear. "We'll catch the devil for this!"

Chapter Thirty

How do you think this is gonna look?" Irving Andrews' booming voice carried around the boardroom. The Denver & Rio Grande and the Denver, South Park & Pacific representatives usually met once a month to discuss the workings of the two railroads, but this was a special meeting called because of recent events in the Arkansas River Valley.

Irv—only his wife called him Irving—enjoyed a reputation as a troubleshooter who got things done. He was also known for his flashy plaid vests and his penchant for good old-fashioned snuff. Some snuff users carried ornate tins, mainly with Oriental designs, and sniffed the powder, only to immediately sneeze most of it out again. Conwood snuff out of Delaware was Irv's brand of choice, and he placed his snuff inside his mouth, using a twig he'd cut off a brush or sapling. He chewed one end until the twig frayed, so all he had to do was put the twig into his mouth and dampen it, put the wet end into his snuff box, and then place it between his lips and gum. He didn't waste it by sneezing, but he did spit a lot. That didn't matter, for Irv loved to be different, so he favored his new way of "dipping" snuff.

"We need to nip this in the bud." He paced the floor while the other men tried to look as if they had a clue as to how to prevent the Flower Gang from jumping one of the scheduled trains that went through Salida, Buena Vista, Leadville, and Fairplay. "We got lucky this time, but the next time this gang won't make the same mistake, and we may not be smiling. They'll strike again, I'll wager."

"We've put extra guards on all the trains. Especially when

112

they have money on them." Samuel Leuderman, a man who made his money racing horses in Salida, pulled his watch from his pleated pants pocket and checked the time. "I've got two fillies coming on today's shipment, so we need to get this business over with before they get here. What's the story on this new sheriff the county hired? I thought he rode hard and was going to be the answer to our problems."

Several of the other men agreed.

"Wagner's just a cowboy from Texas turned lawman," someone said.

Irv motioned for quiet. "He's good, but he's no miracle worker."

The men continued to squabble and get nowhere. Finally Irv had had enough. "I'll talk to the County Commission again. Have them put the pressure on Wagner. They hired him, and they can fire him."

All agreed, and within minutes no one remained in the meeting room.

Irv got results. The next day members of the County Commission confronted Tilman Wagner in his office. They chose to meet there because Butter Pegram always had some of Neala's famous rolls sitting by the coffee. It was a good-sized room, but there was hardly space enough for them all. Tilman and Butter sat quietly, Butter carving a small doll for his youngest while Tilman cleaned a small "Sheriff's Model" Colt he usually kept in the desk drawer.

Commissioner Page, his distrust of Tilman Wagner unchanged, watched with fascination as Tilman twirled the gun on his finger like a Wild West show bad man. "That must have cost a month's pay, Wagner," he said, his eyes betraying a strange combination of envy and fear.

The twirling was all for show, and Page had fallen for it. "Don't know how much it cost, Mr. Page. Belonged to Old Purdy. It's something else, isn't it?" The engraved, nickel-plated gun had a white ivory grip. "Heard he had it special made. I found it in the drawer, so I keep it there in case I need something quick. I prefer my old Colt, since I'm used to it, and it's used to me." He put the gun away. "This one has a three-inch barrel, and that's too small for me."

"You men want some more coffee?" Butter offered. "Maybe one more roll?"

The sheriff's office was much the same as sheriffs' offices all over the West: square, windows on two sides, with the jail in the back. At least Tilman and Butter kept their office clean, and the coffee was always fresh, so several of the men made it a habit to drop by frequently for Neala's rolls. Tilman knew that helped to keep the commissioners on their side.

It was obvious that none of the commissioners wanted to confront Tilman, but something was up, and it wasn't good. Finally Tilman forced the issue. "What can I do for you men? I know you're all busy, so whatever it is, let's get it out in the open and talk about it."

Ray Lewis, the man who had approached Tilman about the sheriff's job, was the commissioner least intimidated by Tilman. He spoke up. "Wagner, we need to know what you're doing about this Flower Gang. That's what the papers are calling them, you know." He tossed a *Rocky Mountain Gazette* onto Tilman's desk. "Have you seen this? They're having a great time at our expense."

Tilman flipped the paper over but didn't look at it. He and Butter had already seen a copy and knew that the commission wasn't going to like it at all.

Lewis continued, "I know you two nearly got killed coming back from Tin Cup last week. Was it the gang?"

"Can't say. What's strange is that, outside of our families, no one but Peel knew we were going." Butter sat down.

The aroma of fresh Arbuckle's coffee wafted through the room, and one of the men murmured, "Aw heck," pushed his chair back, and got a cup and one of Neala's rolls. He was joined by two others.

"Well, something's got to be done. The railroad bosses are jumpy, and when that happens, they land on us. You need to give them something they can see as proof you're going after the gang." The room grew quiet.

"Or what? Do you want my badge, Lewis?" Tilman slowly stood up with one hand on his star, ready to leave.

"Now, Tilman. Don't be hasty." One of the men, a roll in one hand and coffee in the other, stepped between the two men. "We just need something to tell the railroads. They're afraid the next train holdup might actually work."

"They might be right, Mr. Murdock. Butter and I are looking, but about the time we think we've got a handle on this gang, they do something different. The only thing they don't change is leaving the flower. This time of the year I don't even know where they might be getting them. If you have any ideas, we'd be more than happy to hear them."

Ten minutes later the rolls were gone, the coffeepot empty, and the commissioners were gone as well. Butter looked at Tilman. "That was 'much ado about nothing,' as I think Catherine might say."

"You know they're right, Butter. Something has got to change before somebody gets hurt."

Tilman buckled on his old Colt, looked out the window, and grabbed his jacket and gloves. "Turning cold. I'm going over to talk to Marshal Early."

Chapter Thirty-one

Early? You in here?" Tilman stood in the doorway of Tom Early's hotel room. He'd rented two adjoining rooms so he could use one as his office.

"Come on back here." Early's voice came from the other room, and Tilman found him sitting at a table piled with maps and other papers.

"What are you looking for?"

"I have an idea that might pan out, Wagner." Early stood, shook hands, and motioned for Tilman to have a seat. "Thought some of these old papers might have something I could use, but I'd like your opinion."

"How so?"

"Look at this map I got from the railroad. Here." He pointed to several X's penciled on the paper. "Here are the places where the gang has hit so far."

"I see."

"Well, if you look at it closely, they concentrated around Granite and Buena Vista. Could be that their headquarters, if you want to call it that, is right here. Convenient."

"You might have something, Early. Granite, here in town, or somewhere in between."

Tilman waited while Early shuffled and stacked a set of papers. "Heard you had company earlier. The county fire you?"

"No. They're just nervous. This 'Flower Gang,' as they are called, is getting a little too bold for comfort."

"How bad do you want to catch them?"

"You know I do, Early, but I've had precious little to go on."

116

Tilman paused. "Butter and I checked out Marcel Devereaux and a couple of the other new fellows in town. No luck there."

Early nodded. "I have this idea I want to propose to you."

"Let's hear it."

"What do you know about Prosper Charbonneau?"

"His business is a little shady. He actually suggested I turn a blind eye to some things when I first took this job. I can't say he's involved in this, though. He's got his eye set on being respectable. Maybe he'll try his hand at politics, like Tabor, and he doesn't want to do anything to upset that apple cart. Why? You think he might be involved?"

"What about if you told him you want to play his game? Show you might be open to a little exchange of money for your silence." Early leaned back in his chair, waiting.

"Wouldn't work. First, I doubt the offer still stands. Second, that's not something I'd do." Tilman bristled. "You must not know me, Early. I walk a different path. I rode a hard trail for a long time, and when I straightened out, I never wanted to do but what was right."

"Hold on, Wagner. I know who you are. I only meant that maybe you could play it until we heard something that might lead us to the gang."

"My pa told me a man ought to be what he seems to be. I can't change what I am."

"Think about it. That's all. We've got to figure out who's behind this before they kill somebody." Early studied Tilman. He knew that what he was suggesting went against the man's grain. "There may be something to this map. Charbonneau's right here in the middle. Just you think about it."

Chapter Thirty-two

During Pastor Paul Fry's once-a-month church service a cold, blustering north wind came up, sending low clouds flying across the Valley skies. Attendance had been light. After the people went home, the Frys, Pegrams, and Wagners agreed that their planned picnic by the creek ought to be moved inside. It wouldn't do for the babies to get a chill. The men went out to retrieve the baskets of food from their carriages.

Fry came to stand by Tilman and James. "What do you call that thing you're driving?"

"It's a carryall, Pastor." James was eager to tell the preacher about the new light carriage. "A man in Pueblo made it for us."

Butter came to see it. "Three seats, a top, and roll-up sides? Pretty fancy."

"And it's light enough for one horse. Imagine that." Fry climbed aboard to try the comfortable spring seats. "Well, you got room for the young'uns and all their necessaries."

Elbowing the pastor, Butter chaffed Tilman's boy. "I'll bet James will want to drive this when he goes sparkin' all the girls."

James colored while the men took a few more moments to admire the Wagners' new carriage.

After the meal, while the wives began to clean up, the men lingered over their plates and coffee. "Paul, that was some sermon this morning. You had some of them folks just a-shakin'. I'll be glad when you get out of the circuit-riding business so you can be with us every Sunday." Butter sat with the preacher and Tilman while his smallest son ran around and around the men's table. "Little B, quit that. Come sit with your pa for a while." With a grunt he pulled his youngest son onto his lap and placed a drumstick in the boy's hand. "He takes after his pa when it comes to fried chicken and smashed 'taters."

Paul Fry deadpanned, "Now that you mention it, he *is* a chunky little fellow. Is that what you mean?"

Butter patted his growing middle while the men laughed. Little B, holding the drumstick in one hand, happily plucked another piece of chicken from Butter's plate.

Fry pushed himself back from the table. "Say, Tilman, not to ruin a perfectly good dinner, but is there any news on this gang of thieves, the ones they call the Flower Gang?"

"No, not a bit. It's a puzzle to me. Usually after a holdup or robbery some fellow without two dimes to rub together shows up bragging and throwing around a lot of money. Or else he'll load up on whiskey and start bragging." Tilman shook his head. "Not this time, though. Marshal Early has had no more luck then we have. I'm not sure what to do."

The pastor placed his empty cup on the table. "Do you think it was the Flower Gang that tried to stop that train last week?"

Butter wiped Little B's face and then sent him off to go find his mother. "We don't know who that was. They couldn't catch the train to leave their calling card."

"What's this about trains?" Catherine came in, pushing the twins in their new Heywood Brothers rattan carriage. It had recently been delivered, a gift from Esperanza, David Stone's wife and Catherine's sister-in-law, in New Mexico. Although the Stones were family, they felt they owed Tilman because he had stamped out a gang trying to steal their cattle and take over their ranch. "They're sound asleep. Isn't this the most amazing carriage?"

"Yup."

"That's a fact."

Butter and the pastor offered obligatory but unenthusiastic responses. Tilman alone managed a halfway sincere, "It sure is." The twins were dead to the world, so he'd have said much the same if they'd been in an old milk wagon. "A little fancy for my taste, but Esperanza's girls think Catherine hung the moon. For that matter, so do I." Tilman blushed, Pastor Fry laughed, and Butter grinned.

"You're getting real smooth, Tilman." Catherine hugged her husband. He was a man of few words, but she knew where she stood in his heart.

"We're all packed and ready for you men to load up." Minna, Paul's wife of two years, and Butter's wife, Neala, joined the group, Little B on her hip, dozing. "We don't have a lot of left-overs."

Minna had been a late addition to the group. A widow for several years, she and Paul had married after a brief court-ship, and neither had looked back since. The three couples had shared joys, heartaches, and life with one another over the years, and now they were like a family in many ways.

Minna sat beside her husband while her friend remained standing. "Neala, why don't you tell them your news?"

Butter reached out to take Little B from his mama's arms. "What is it? We're not expecting another, are we, little woman?" They all laughed at Butter's pet name for Neala, because he stood a good six inches shorter than she, and his friends loved to josh him. He took it in stride.

"Oh, no, Mister Pegram. It's not that at all!"

"Aw." Butter wasn't sure if he should be disappointed or relieved.

With barely concealed pride, she went on. "I've been asked by the Ladies' Circle to represent all the churches in the Val-ley at the big baking contest in Colorado Springs at the Broad-leaf Hotel."

Paul Fry leaped to his feet and clapped his hands. "Hurrah!" The others joined in the applause. Neither Tilman nor Butter saw through Paul's exuberance to catch on to the fact that he already knew about the contest.

"Bully for you, Aunt Neala!" James stood to give her a hug.

Neala continued, "Now, it's next week, and I know that's awful short notice, but Minna's already offered to keep our two oldest. Catherine said she'd go with me to help me prepare, and she can keep an eye on the little ones." Her face broke into an ear-to-ear smile. "Can you imagine? Me?"

Butter recovered his composure. "Of course I can, silly woman." He reached up to kiss her. "After all, you caught *me* with your cinnamon rolls. Ain't that what you're gonna fix?"

Tilman and Butter were oblivious to all the planning the ladies had already done. While the others closed around to congratulate Neala, Catherine turned to Tilman. "Is it all right with you if I go with her, Tilman? She can't cook and manage Little B and Sis. We'll be back before you miss us."

"It's fine, Catherine. Now's a good time, before winter comes and closes the passes."

"Tilman, I'll take the twins, and we'll be fine." Catherine turned to look at Neala. "She is so excited. I think she has a good chance of winning the contest."

"Do they award medals to the winner?"

"I don't know about medals," she said, "but the grand prize is one hundred dollars!"

Tilman nodded and whistled appreciatively.

"We'll be back by Tuesday afternoon on the D&RG."

"You've already looked at the train schedules? Say, how long have you three been planning this?" Butter held up his hands in resignation. "Never mind. I know when I've been outfoxed!"

Tilman couldn't help but agree. This would be a grand adventure for the two women. Besides, Catherine and the twins' absence would give him more time to look for the Flower Gang.

"Best we get home. I need to help James with the chores before it gets dark. That is, if James is ready to leave the ladies." He pointed with his chin to where his son, sixteen years old and a head taller than most of the other boys his age, stood with three young girls who had "happened" to drop by the church. James was a hard worker and a good student. Next year they planned on sending him off to school. He wanted to go to Texas A&M to study agriculture and maybe become an animal doctor. "How he plans on leaving the girls behind and going to college is going to be something to see."

Chapter Thirty-three

The dim pools of yellow light cast by coal-oil lamps along Main Street became islands in the darkness. After a day of blustery high winds that finally stilled after sunset, the night grew cold. From the Roundhouse Saloon came the sound of men talking and singing along with a lively player-piano rendition of "The Daring Young Man on the Flying Trapeze." On the boardwalk outside the saloon two men half carried, half dragged an argumentative drunk between them, his arms draped over their shoulders. They crossed the street and entered the D&RG work crews' bunkhouse beside the station, and the night became quiet but for the sharp clicks of hoofbeats on the hard-packed road.

The little mare knew her way home, and Marcel Devereaux sat easy on the runabout's comfortably padded leather seat, the reins loose in his hand. The little carriage's canvas top was up, and, carelessly, Marcel had forgotten to light the headlamp mounted outside on the right corner of the dashboard. The street lamps ended on the other side of Railroad Avenue where the street crossed Cottonwood Creek, and the darkness deepened. With little to attract his attention, Marcel recalled Marie Fleur's insistence that she'd be in charge of the details of the next plan to rob a train. His face burned with humiliation as he recalled her fury when their first attempt at a train robbery had failed miserably. What did she know about stopping a train?

A figure lunged from the darkness into the street, and the mare swerved in fright. The animal stopped, reared with eyes rolling white in the dark, but a second man appeared to grab her bridle and hold it fast. The sudden stop in the darkness so surprised Marcel, he almost lost his seat. "You there, release my horse!"

The first man approached Marcel. "If you're heeled, don't go for it. I got a message for you."

"I'm not armed. If it's money you want, you've got the wrong man."

"This ain't a stickup, bub." The man's arm shot out, and a strong hand grabbed Marcel by the front of his coat, throwing him into the street, where he landed on his belly. He tasted dust, but even before he could spit, the night exploded with stars when the dark figure delivered a hard kick to his midsection.

"This is the message, bub. The boys in Leadville said you're runnin' outta time." That same strong hand hauled Marcel to his feet and held him erect while with his other hand the man slapped Marcel's face, hard, first with open palm, next with the back of his hand.

The man holding the horse called to the man holding Marcel. "Hey, the boss said not to mark him up!"

"Yeah, I hear you." The man shifted his attack back to Marcel's midsection. "I'll not mess up his pretty face."

In stunned helplessness, Marcel absorbed blow after blow from the man's fists, trying to bend over while raising one knee in a useless attempt to ward off more punches to his belly. Marcel was twelve years old when last he had been in a fight with another boy. He had no idea how to handle himself in a street brawl. "Please . . . ," he managed to gasp before a final hard blow to his middle knocked the breath out of him.

The man let go of his coat, and Marcel collapsed in the street, retching, gasping for breath.

"Let this be a warning, bub. If you don't come up with the money, next time we won't end it here."

Marcel managed to raise himself to his hands and knees. His head hung low, a string of bloody saliva dripping from his chin.

"D'you get me?"

Marcel nodded. But suddenly he was alone. He slowly climbed to the high-backed leather seat of the runabout. His fingers probed the darkness of the passenger seat. The oilskin wallet he'd tossed there at the office was still there. Relief flooded over him. Those men had said they weren't robbers, but if they'd known about the wallet, well, you could never trust toughs like them. That kind of man would steal without hesitation and swear otherwise.

The irony of his thoughts never occurred to him.

Later, after he'd slipped quietly into his room at his uncle's house, Marcel splashed water from a pitcher into the wash-stand bowl, soaked a washcloth, and held it to his face. "It could have been worse," he said aloud to his reflection in the mirror. His face was reddened from the open-handed blows. With the first two fingers of his right hand he pulled down his tender lower lip to see how badly he was cut. The lip was swollen, but the cut was inside. It had bled profusely but was, after all, only a small cut. The mirror showed he was not marked, but with any movement his ribs ached painfully. He winced. Whoever had hit him had fists like iron.

He poured himself a drink and sat in an overstuffed chair in his bedroom, the wallet in his lap. Prosper had trusted him with the safe's combination, for, after all, Marcel was family. To Prosper's way of thinking, family didn't steal from family. Marcel had stayed late after his uncle left the downtown office above the bank, and he'd taken only enough money to pay off his Leadville debt. After they robbed the train, he'd put back the money, and no one would be the wiser. He took a drink, but the fiery liquor seared his cut lip, so he spat the liquor back into the glass. "Humph."

A wave of fear came over him. The danger of his situation became clear. If anything should go wrong, those men would come back. Marcel did not want to die. He had to get the gang together to move quickly. They'd have to stop a train and get into the express car. Maybe Marie Fleur could find a way. He'd see what kind of plan she could make. It would have to be soon, for those men would certainly kill him next time.

Chapter Thirty-four

Have you ever seen anything so beautiful?" Neala stood in the center of the large foyer of the Broadleaf Hotel in the foothills of Pikes Peak in Colorado Springs. The white marble interior was both stark and grand. The floors were a rich, deep red and white checkerboard marble. Fresh flowers from the large greenhouse in back of the hotel filled the room, the blue of hydrangeas, pale phlox, and fresh red roses making a sharp contrast of colors.

"One lady told me that they have a staff of fifty to take care of the flowers alone. It's really unbelievable." Catherine couldn't help but admire the beauty around her, yet she knew that the money spent on that greenhouse would probably feed a small town. "What would it be like to be so wealthy?"

"I can't imagine, but what a wonderful place for a cooking contest." Neala and Catherine quietly watched the other women from all parts of the state entering the building, noting the ones with bags of homemade ingredients and a favorite pan or two lovingly carried in a worn tote bag.

Two solidly corseted wasp-waisted ladies attired in the latest clothing fashions from New York gave them a wide berth, and one of them, severely prim, audibly sniffed. The other of the upper-crust ladies placed her handkerchief to her nose as they swept past Neala and Catherine, surrounded by their expedition baggage and cluster of small children.

Neala turned to watch them hurry out of the room. "What was that all about?"

Catherine looked down at a stain on her jacket, a gift from one of the twins. "I suppose I must smell like sour milk."

Neala looked at Catherine and then broke into a grin. "I hope they aren't around if the two little ones bust loose. They'd really be insulted!"

"I just hope those two aren't the judges. Here," Catherine said as she motioned to the hotel clerk, "let's get these children upstairs to our room, and then we can rest and bathe and get ready for dinner."

The room they shared was spacious, and there was plenty of freedom for the children to roam. Tired from the trip, the little ones were soon asleep, while Catherine and Neala checked to see that they had all the ingredients they might need.

Neala had a sudden attack of worry about the morrow. "I had to adjust my baking powder for the Valley because it's so high. Down in Texas I didn't need as much powder. I hope the recipe will work the same here as at home."

Catherine nodded agreement. She understood that Neala was nervous and only thinking out loud. Neala was as unshakeable as a rock most of the time. This was a side of her friend that Catherine had never seen. Cattle rustlers couldn't faze the tall woman, but the prospect of having strangers judge her cooking clearly intimidated Neala.

Catherine took Neala's hand. "Don't worry, you'll be fine. Act as if you're cooking something for Butter."

A knock sounded on the door, and a young woman called from outside. "Mrs. Pegram?"

Neala looked at Catherine and opened the door. "That would be me."

Standing in the hallway was a businesslike young lady, pince-nez glasses perched on her nose, hair in a tight bun, dressed in a white blouse and black skirt. "Good evening." She stepped into the room. "My name is Miss Malone. I'm here to watch the children while you eat supper in the main dining room with the other contestants." Neala stared in wonder. Miss Malone quickly crossed the room to check on the children. She found them asleep, so she sat down on the sofa, opened a copy of *Godey's Magazine and Lady's Book,* and said, "Enjoy your supper," and she proceeded to read.

"Well, isn't that a nice surprise." Catherine smiled and got her light coat. "Come on before she realizes she has the wrong room." Neala joined her at the door. "Send a bellman to page us if you have a problem."

The young woman, magazine in hand, waved them out the door. "I won't have a problem."

The winding stairway was filled with women on their way to the dining room. Several couples were mixed in among the crowd, but they were evidently used to staying at the elegant hotel and didn't appear to notice the others. The rich red velvet carpet made a quiet statement against the gleaming teak banisters.

"I'm glad Little B isn't with us. He'd dearly love to slide down these rails."

While their clothing was not designer made, and their complexions were those of women who were no strangers to the windy and sunny high country, the two still drew appreciative looks from some of the traveling men who lounged in the downstairs lobby enjoying a drink with their newspapers. Neala was tall, slim, and fair, while Catherine was softer looking with reddish-blond hair and hazel eyes that reflected an inner peace. The two were western women who had remained women in spite of the rough country they were working to help tame. Neala wore a light blue travel dress with a small bustle, and Catherine wore a pale green two-piece travel outfit that also had a small bustle. Neither wore a hat, and both women had their hair in braids that framed their faces.

The *maître d'hôtel* asked their names and with a snap of his fingers had the headwaiter escort them into the dining room to their table and ensure that servers attended them. The ladies they sat with were from the mining town of Creede, and they were soon talking like old friends. The kitchen door swung back and forth as waiters in black and white served. The first course was an appetizer of raw or baked oysters. The second course featured a choice of two cream soups or plain bouillon along with a serving of baked or broiled fish. Then came the main course—roasted poultry, pork, or beef, accompanied by a variety of savory vegetables and freshly baked bread.

The ladies met each course with barely suppressed delight, for the food was tasty and wonderfully presented. The dessert course began with several puddings, cakes, and highly prized specialties such as Nesselrode and plum pudding. A variety of cheeses and fresh fruit were available as well to clean the palate. Hot rolls and coffee or tea were continuously refilled. Dessert ended with fresh ice cream with chocolate sauce on pound cake.

"If I eat another bite, I think I'll burst." Catherine held her hands over her stomach. "I don't know when I have eaten so much and enjoyed it so."

Murmured agreement came from around the table. After a short welcoming speech came a program of singing and a recitation, and then the guests retired to get ready for the next day's activities. Arriving back at their room, Neala and Catherine found the children still asleep. The young woman looking after them was asleep as well, her magazine open beside her.

"I imagine she had a long day." Catherine gently touched the girl, gave her a small tip, and closed the door behind her. "What a wonderful day."

Their morning started early. Behind the hotel a row of splendidly decorated circus tents, each representing a different section of the state, contained tables for each contestant. Opposite the tents were open-sided huts—actually, converted toolsheds—housing wood-fired Stanley ranges, although some contestants asked to use the hotel's cooking ranges. It was an ambitious enterprise, the first of its kind in the state. Neala found her table and set to work. A noon deadline marked the start of the judging. Throughout the busy morning Neala heard occasional shrieks of despair from unfortunate contestants, which could only mean a favorite recipe had failed for lack of a key ingredient, inactive yeast, or an oven too hot or not hot enough. At last a red-faced Neala presented her cinnamon rolls for competition.

A light snow drifted down from the clouds hiding Pikes Peak. Catherine tried not to think about the train ride back across the mountains the next morning. Why worry? Autumn snows could be bad but were usually a problem only on the higher peaks. She had four little ones to keep her busy, so there was no time to think about the weather. By afternoon the skies were clear and calm.

The same young woman who had looked after the children on the first night appeared at their door promptly at supper-time, and the two women joined the other contestants, who were all anxious to see who would take home a prize. Most of the prizes to be awarded were five or ten dollars with two twenty-five dollar prizes, but the winner of the grand prize would take home one hundred dollars. Tension fairly hummed around the dining room the way air vibrates before a lightning strike. The sponsors of the contest, expecting that appetites would fall victim to nervousness, did not attempt to duplicate the previous evening's meal. Tonight a large ham with scalloped potatoes and corn fritters was served, followed with cherries jubilee for dessert.

"I'm glad the contest ends tonight, or I'd have to ride the train home standing up." Catherine pushed her plate away as Neala sighed and tried to loosen the button on her slim skirt.

"May I have your attention, please?" Eldon Jarvis, Master of Ceremonies, was the co-owner of Celestial Flours in Denver. He called everyone to attention, and except for a few nervous titters it became very quiet in the large dining room. As the awards were called out, Neala and Catherine quietly anticipated the naming of the desserts. A prize would go a long way for shoes and winter coats for the family. "Mrs. Patterson of Creede wins the prize for best dessert for her irresistible brownies in clotted cream." Applause followed, and Neala whispered to Catherine, "They were wonderful. I ate two and asked her for the recipe."

Catherine patted Neala's hand. "Well, the trip alone was a prize for me."

"I agree. I don't know when I . . ." Neala realized that the lady on her other side was tapping on her shoulder.

"Mrs. Pegram. They're calling your name."

"What?"

On the speaker's dais, the man from Denver caught her eye, motioning her to the front of the room.

Neala made her way to the stage.

"Here she comes, ladies, our Grand Cook-off champion and winner of the hundred-dollar top prize, Mrs. Neala Pegram of Nathrop! Her cinnamon rolls won hands-down. In fact, the judges asked me not to say anything, but of the three dozen submitted for judging"—Mr. Jarvis held up a dish containing a single bun—"here is the only one left!" Sedate applause gave way to cheers and even a loud whistle.

Neala held the check, still in shock while a photographer set up his flash tray to take her picture.

Catherine rushed to her side to hug her friend. "What will Butter say to that?"

"Who?" Mr. Jarvis looked around.

"Butter is Mr. Pegram, my husband."

"That's an unusual name. Why, of course he'll be pleased as punch."

The evening wound down, and soon Neala and Catherine made their way back up to the room to prepare to leave early in the morning.

Daylight found the snow melted and the two women and four children ready to return home. The little ones had behaved well enough but were missing their yards and roaming room. At the station, Catherine noticed several extra guards with guns around the express car at the boarding platform and commented on them to Neala.

"I'll bet there's a payroll on this trip."

"All aboard!" the train conductor called. Up in the locomotive cab, the engineer reached up to his pull cord and gave one long blast on the locomotive's steam whistle, paused, and gave another long blast to signal that he'd released the brakes.

The ladies and children started for home.

Chapter Thirty-five

Neala Pegram settled into a comfortable armchair across the aisle from Catherine in the nearly new Pullman railroad car. "This luxury"—she made a sweeping motion of her right hand, taking in their unaccustomed surroundings—Turkish carpet, draperies, plush red velvet cushioned reclining chairs, paintings above the windows, shiny, lacquered wood—"is sinful. You are a daring woman, Catherine, tempting me with such worldly delights. Why didn't you tell me?"

A grinning Catherine inclined her head to look at Neala. "It's our little secret. You won't believe this, but Pastor Fry suggested we return on the Midland instead of going back the way we came through Pueblo."

"But why?" Neala's practical side led her to watch every nickel. "This seems a bit extravagant for plain folks."

Catherine's eyes sparkled with excitement when, with a jerk, the train began to roll and left the Colorado Springs station below Pikes Peak for the short pull to Manitou Springs. "Pastor Fry assured me that the price of our tickets would be nearly the same. The prices are low to attract business." She opened a colorfully printed *Colorado Midland Railroad Official Timetable and Connections* brochure with illustrations featuring a snowy mountain scene and a snarling mountain lion. "The Midland's passenger service to Buena Vista started only last week. See?" She pointed to the route. "Our new route goes up Ute Pass through Divide, Florissant, Hartsel—all places I've never seen but I've read about. We still end up at the new depot on Free Gold Hill at Buena Vista. Why not see the country in style?"

131

A look of confusion clouded Neala's face. "But the rail-road's not finished up there. They're still blasting tunnels and building bridges across the gorges at Four Mile north of town."

Catherine leaned close to Neala and patted her hand to re-assure her friend. "Don't be afraid. Tilman told me just the other day that he rode up the new trail the Midland cut from the depot down to the bridge, over the river, and into town for freight and passengers. He said it's like a small town up there, with a depot, storage sheds, a section house, cookhouse, and a bunkhouse for workers. The road's steep, but wagons and a celerity manage nicely, so it'll be another adventure for us."

A porter set a steaming pot of tea and a platter of small cakes at one of the tables and then held the chairs for Cathe-rine and Neala, who, in spite of her no-nonsense outlook on life, fell victim to Catherine's almost girlish excitement. The twins and Neala's two little ones slept soundly. The hotel had been a wonderful adventure, but it had worn them all out, es-pecially the children. The car was only partly filled, their seven fellow travelers remaining at the other end of the car.

"Did you notice that the other passengers chose to sit at the far end of the car?" Catherine motioned with one hand. "I wonder if these four little ones are who we should be thanking for the extra room at this end."

The two friends laughed as they enjoyed the semiprivacy of the spacious car. Time passed while they alternated between happy conversations and playing the role of sightseers.

Crossing the pass at Divide, where the train stopped briefly, they felt the air grow chilly, with thick clouds darkening the route ahead. Soon a porter passed out lap blankets, while an-other adjusted gratings for the new steam-heating system. The temperature inside the car quickly returned to a comfortable level. But once again Neala voiced her concern about the threat-ening weather.

"You'll get used to it. Our weather in the high country is unpredictable, but never more so than during the autumn. I'll bet we'll see snow before we get home!" Catherine pressed her face to the window to watch the gathering clouds. It did look like the weather might be about to change at any minute.

Neala's eyes widened with apprehension. West Texas weather could be just as bad, but at least there she'd known what to expect. "Mr. Pegram was determined to come back to live here, and I'll live where he wants me to, but this Colorado country is going to take some getting used to."

By midafternoon the train was making only slow progress. On the flat plain between the mining camps at Spinney and Hartsel the wind blew the tracks clear of snow, while past Hartsel the engine labored through drifts several feet deep. The train slowed to a crawl when climbing to almost ten thousand feet to reach Trout Creek Pass in near-whiteout conditions, the cars swaying in the buffeting winds.

"Oh my, Catherine." Neala watched the large white flakes as they floated down onto the tracks. "I hope we are soon out of this storm."

"Me too, Neala." Catherine now held Carson, the stronger of the twins and the one who equated eating with breathing. Descending, the train picked up speed, and they felt that the worst was over. Soon they passed the little station at Newett without stopping. The grade twisted and turned, following the contours of the rugged terrain as it descended in the lee of the Mosquito Mountains. The going became easier beneath a darkly threatening sky and building winds. Catherine and Neala became hopeful that the snow would abate in the short time remaining until they arrived at the Buena Vista depot.

By the time the train passed below the eight-thousand-foot level, the storm showed signs of blowing itself out. Most of the snow had stopped falling. The afternoon sun setting over the mountain peaks forming the western wall of the Arkansas River Valley cast bursts of color between flying thick clouds to illuminate the valley floor. When the grade swung northward on the lower slopes of Free Gold Hill, now called Midland Hill, Neala could see Buena Vista. "Why, there's hardly any snow in town!"

Catherine stood so she could see the town, then staggered

and almost fell as a wind gust rocked the car. "What a grand sight!"

"Perhaps the worst of the storm struck high in the mountains and spared the town."

"We're nearly home." Catherine breathed a silent thanks to God for delivering them safely.

The two began gathering up hand luggage, toys, blankets, and the picnic hamper that had served so well to pacify the children.

Chapter Thirty-six

The climb up Midland Hill was more difficult than they had expected because of the storm lashing the peaks above them with high winds and snow. Marcel, riding in front, swung his mount off the trail. "Here's where we make our own way."

Marie Fleur followed, grasping her saddle horn as her horse climbed steeply, struggling for footing. "But aren't we near the top? Why do we have to leave the pathway?"

"They'll see us if we get any closer to the depot."

They rode in silence, glad now that the wind came from behind rather than into their faces. Soon they climbed onto the level railroad grade, where the snow lay several feet deep but the going became somewhat easier. "Stay close to the sides," Lars urged. "Your hoss'll tangle in them rails and cross ties if you don't." Lars and his brother, Cooter, looked alike, but Lars seemed the more prepared. Cooter acted as if he wasn't sure where he was most of the time. But he loved playing with dynamite and matches and fireworks, so he was perfect for his line of work.

Marcel studied the place Marie Fleur had chosen to stop the train. They were less than a mile south of the station, where the train would be rounding a sharp curve bordered by a thirty-foot drop to a shelf below. Above the cut was a steep slope. He looked with concern at a thick snowbank at the crest. He shuddered to think what would happen if an avalanche caught them there.

Cooter pointed to a small shed on a ledge near the tracks. "Yonder's where I stashed the blasting powder." He dismounted and waded through the snow to the shed. He emerged with a tied bundle of eight-inch-long sticks of Hercules Blasting Powder in one hand and a coil of ropy black fuse in the other.

"Don't forget the blasting caps," Marie Fleur said.

Cooter touched the hand with the fuse to his coat pocket. "Got a box of 'em right here."

Marcel became apprehensive. He knew nothing about explosives. That was something he left to the rough miners who lived in the districts around Buena Vista. "Do you mean to blow up the train?"

"Naw, I'm just gonna make a hole in the tracks."

"Does it take that many sticks to do it? Is that not too much?" Marcel asked. He turned from Cooter to place a hand on his cousin's arm. "Marie Fleur, is this your idea of how to make the train stop?"

"Cooter has worked in the mines. He knows how to do this. Show him, Cooter."

Marcel watched as the man knelt in the snow. Lars opened a narrow blade in his pocketknife and passed it down to Cooter, who used the blade to punch a hole in one end of the center stick of explosive. He tossed the dynamite bundle up to Lars, who yelled, "Boom!" and startled Marcel. A laughing Cooter then used the blade to cut off a foot-long piece of fuse. He pulled a wooden box of blasting caps from his pocket, slid the top back, and extracted a shiny silver tube about an inch long and open on one end. He split one end of the fuse and inserted the other end into the cap opening.

Lars poked Marcel's shoulder. "Now for some fun."

Marcel winced. "What is he going to do now?"

"Well, we hope he ain't gonna blow his teeth out."

"The boys in the mines use a crimping tool. If you ain't got one, this'll do." Cooter raised the fused cap and stuck it into his mouth.

The sight of a man about to blow his head off transfixed Marie Fleur. In spite of herself she couldn't turn her eyes away. What a fascinating thing!

With a hideous mockery of a grin Cooter set his front teeth at the end of the cap where the fuse entered and bit down gently, thus crimping the cap tightly around the fuse so it wouldn't come loose from the mercury fulminate in the cap that would detonate the blasting powder. He removed it, then studied it to see if the crimp would hold. "That's it."

Lars gave the dynamite bundle back to Cooter, who kicked snow away from the rails and found a place where two rail ends met, an expansion space between them held open by an iron fishplate bolting the rails into place. Lars dismounted to help. He raked crushed rock ballast away, and Cooter stuck the bundle into the depression. Finally he poked the capped fuse into the hole he'd made in the center stick of dynamite. "Ready to go."

Marie Fleur pulled a pocket watch from her coat. The train should be coming along anytime now. "We'll wait."

But an hour passed before the faint sound of a train whistle sounded. "They're coming," Marie Fleur said. "It's about time. Cooter, get over there, and be ready."

"*Chérie*," Marcel said, "they're closer than you think. The wind is blowing the sound away from us."

Marie Fleur pointed back up the tracks toward the station to a mound of snow covering heaped excavation spoil. "We'll go behind that and wait until the train stops. Then we'll make our move. Light it, Cooter!"

Marcel's voice trembled. "I hope you know what you're doing, cousin."

Cooter cupped a burning match in his hand against the wind and held the flame to the end of the fuse. With a jet of smoke and flame the fuse ignited, its blue smoke torn away on the wind. He dropped the fuse end and waddled through the snow toward the place where the others held their horses in safety. He stood still for a moment and watched the flame race down the fuse.

Marie Fleur shouted to the others, "Get your bandannas over your faces! Cooter, get over here!"

Hardly had Cooter joined them when the train rounded the bend, headlamp glowing. The others craned their necks to see, but Lars, fingers pressed into his ears, ducked behind the spoil.

Their view of the train disappeared in a sharp *wham* from a flash of flame and a spray of snow, ballast rock, black smoke, and debris. A six-foot section of track was destroyed, one end of a rail curled upward and back on itself to form a grotesque letter *C,* while the other bent crazily to the side. Their horses danced in fear, tugging at the reins, barely under control.

Cooter gave a surprised grunt when a heavy iron fishplate smashed into his chest and threw him backward. His horse bolted and ran toward the station. The sound of the blast echoed across the valley, mixing with the shrill steel-on-steel squeal of brakes, the continuous scream of the train whistle drowning out Cooter's final gasp. Marcel saw the man fall but was torn, looking from Cooter to the slow-motion approach of the train to the broken track and back again.

Marie Fleur whispered, "*Mon Dieu.*"

The massive engine pushed the bent rail aside with a sickening lurch as its momentum carried it to the small crater. Driven by the weight of the cars behind it, the engine tipped left, the cowcatcher plowing debris. The leading bogie wheels sheared and were run over by the drive wheels when the engine slid over the lip and down the slope. All three robbers watched in horror as the engine came to rest on the lip of the cliff, clouds of white steam erupting from broken boiler pipes.

Lars saw the engineer and fireman leap from the cab, landing uphill from the still-sliding engine. "They made it out!"

The tender followed the engine, tipping over and spilling coal. To Marcel, the sounds of the wreck were lost in the terror of actually watching it happen. "Here comes the express car!" But the sound of his voice was lost as the car splintered on impact with the back of the tender.

The noise ended as suddenly as it had started. The only sound was the hissing of steam escaping the engine. The back half of the train—a Pullman car and two chair cars with a caboose attached—remained on the tracks. Passengers had thrown open windows and leaned out to see. Farther back, several men had dismounted from the chair cars but, seeing the masked robbers, fearfully held back.

Marcel was suddenly elated. "It worked! We have our train."

Marie Fleur stared in disbelief. "Cousin, I think you're

crazy, but it does look like we have stopped this mighty beast right in its tracks." She looked around. "Let's get moving. We don't have much time. They probably heard the noise in Buena Vista, maybe even Leadville."

Before Marcel could answer, Lars finally turned to find Cooter dead behind them. "No! My brother's dead!"

Their attention was drawn to movement in and around the wreckage. The fireman half carried a limping engineer up to the tracks. In the tangle that had been the express car, the messenger, cradling his broken right arm, picked his way out.

Marcel pointed at a padlocked chest. "See? The money box! Come on!"

Marie passed her reins to Lars. "Hold the horses!" Lars stared at his dead brother but held the others' horses. Grief wasn't big in his family. He and Cooter rode together, but he wouldn't waste time mourning him. Life was just that. Here and then gone.

Marcel and Marie hurried to the wreck and climbed down. Marcel pulled the chest from the debris. Marie Fleur stood back as Marcel tried to lift it. "Careful, Marcel! It's heavy!" She handed him her gun. "Here. Shoot off the padlock."

"Stand back." Marcel took aim, and one shot split the lock. He handed Marie her gun, then bent and flipped open the lid to reveal a fortune in gold and silver coins and banded stacks of paper money. Marie helped him cram the gold and silver into their saddlebags.

Marie's bandanna had fallen, unnoticed. Her eyes were shining with excitement. She had pulled this robbery off, and she had saddlebags of gold and silver coins to prove it. In the fever of the moment she heard someone speak to her.

"Marie Fleur? Is that you?"

At the sound of a familiar voice, Marie Fleur turned to see who had called out to her. She was shocked to see a pale and shaking Catherine Wagner standing on the Pullman car's open platform. Marie yelled, "Go back inside!" Unthinking, she pulled her gun and waved it. "Go back!"

Only too late did she understand that Catherine recognized her and that now everyone would know. As she tried to put her mask back on, she heard a strange roaring sound coming from the mountain above the train.

A rumbling *whoosh* came next, growing louder when a rushing wall of snow and small trees, billowing into fine mist, bore down on the scene at the wreck. The stream-cut terrain channeled the slide down a V-shaped draw above them. Close by, the draw widened into a bowl at the point where the rail bed, built on spoil taken from a cut, crossed it. The bowl absorbed much of the avalanche's energy, yet it retained sufficient force when it smashed against the train to shove the cars from the tracks.

The avalanche Marcel feared was now a nightmarish reality, but a reality that spared his life by merely brushing past him. "Run! Run!" Carrying both saddlebags, Marcel struggled back to the place where Lars held their horses, and he swung the bags across the saddle of his horse. "We've got to get out of here!" He climbed aboard and spurred his mount through the snow, never looking to see if the others followed.

"What about the people on the train?" Marie Fleur called. "They might need help!" Marie Fleur and Lars were close behind him.

"Marie Fleur, we just robbed their train, and we have to get away. There will be help from the town soon. They'll be fine. But if they find us, we'll hang, I promise you. Come on. Let's ride."

Marie Fleur didn't dare look back to see if Catherine Wagner was still standing in the Pullman. Surely she'd gone back inside. Marie Fleur and the others rode hard, leaving the carnage behind.

Chapter Thirty-seven

Tilman sat at his desk, looking at a page of figures. Butter busied himself sweeping the office and emptying the trash, not that any of it needed to be done, but simply to mask his concern. "That mail hack driver, did he say when the station-master thought the train was coming in?"

Tilman glanced at the wall clock. "Soon, I think."

"Any word yet?" Pastor Fry came to the door. "I'm eager to hear about that new car the ladies rode on. I'd hoped they'd be here by now."

"Nope, nothing yet. I think Butter and I are going to ride on up to the depot to be there when they arrive. Why don't you ride along with us?"

"It's cold, and that wind is fierce, but I don't mind if I do. Minna and the kids are at the church doing some work in the hall, so I have some time. She says I get in the way if I'm there."

By late afternoon the snow had stopped, but the wind contin-ued to push down the sun-mottled valley. They were nearing the bridge at the foot of Free Gold Hill when they heard a sound like thunder from the railroad cut high on the hill above them. Hard on the heels of that sound came the scream of a locomotive whistle. Butter turned to Tilman, both men stunned by the noise. "What the devil?"

Pastor Fry quickly breathed a prayer to his Maker while looking in the direction of the sound. "This wind plays tricks on you, but it came from south of the depot, I think. They wouldn't still be blasting down there, would they?"

The men spurred across the trembling bridge as the train's whistle ended, but then came a rumbling crash that seemed to go on and on. Brakes screamed, getting louder and louder; the train whistle sounded one last time, briefly, and then stopped. From where the men were, down the mountain, the hiss of escaping steam echoed over the din, then faded into silence.

"The train's wrecked!" Tilman hauled back on the reins, his horse dancing on the narrow road cut into the side of the hill. "Paul, will you go back and get help? We'll go on up there, but you get back as soon as you can!"

Pastor Fry nodded and wheeled his horse to head back down the hill. Tilman hated to ask him, as they all knew a man of the cloth would be needed if there were seriously injured people. Paul didn't shy from death, but it was always painful to say good-bye. He had ridden both sides of faith, and the man he now was had found a reassuring inner peace. Tilman knew he'd be back.

Short minutes later the sounds of an avalanche came from the direction of the wreck. Although the two men couldn't see the snow slide, the sound of rocks crashing, the noise of the weight of the snow pushing down trees reached their ears, and they looked up to see a cloud of white mist dancing and swirling above the mountains farther down the tracks.

Tilman and Butter soon climbed to the Midland Depot, coming onto a scene of confused activity. The work crews had been mustered from the bunkhouse, and men were pushing down the tracks, where a column of steam and smoke was whipped above the trees by the wind. Four men lifted a handcar onto the rails, leaped aboard, and pumped furiously to follow the rescuers. Tilman recognized the stationmaster on the platform. "How bad is it?"

"Can't tell yet!"

"What was that explosion?"

"Sounded like blasting powder, but the boys aren't working today."

"I'm heading down there—my wife and babies are on that train. When the preacher gets here, tell him where we are."

"Wagner, you men be careful. That was an avalanche,

probably caused by the explosion, and it's somewhere around that bend."

The pealing of several church bells came on the wind from the town down below. The firehouse bell joined in, the agreed-upon emergency call to Buena Vista's able-bodied men to come ready to help. Tilman and Butter rode beside the curving tracks, afraid to hurry lest they cripple their horses on the tracks, cross ties, and ballast rocks under the snow. The ride wasn't long, but progress was agonizingly slow as the two men picked their way around the scattered chunks of rubble blasted loose in the explosion. A spill now could be fatal.

"Can't you go any faster?" Tilman tried to guide his horse around the depot's rescue wagon as it made its way along the tracks. The rail bed here was a narrow ledge cut into the side of the mountain, leaving little room for anything to pass the wagon. It was dangerous in the best of times, and the heavy snow didn't help.

An audible gasp escaped Tilman's lips at the terrible scene before him. The train was mostly on its side off the tracks downhill on a natural shelf, the cars partially buried under snow. Dazed passengers, some bloodied and injured, others seeming unharmed, wandered around the wreckage. Leaving Butter behind, he hurried to a small group of men clustered around two fellows in railroader's overalls, one of whom had been scalded by escaping steam and moaned in pain. Tilman saw but did not comprehend a blackened crater breaking the rails. As his horse slid to a stop, Tilman left the saddle. "Where's the Pullman?"

One of the men pointed to a car tilted at a crazy angle behind a tangle of broken wood and metal that had been the express car. The duties of sheriff forgotten, Tilman could think only of his wife and children trapped, maybe dead, below him. Tilman slid down the hill. "Catherine! Neala! Where are you?"

"Wagner!"

Tilman turned to see Butter whipping and spurring his horse down the tracks to join him. Butter never mistreated a mount, but today he'd stop at nothing to get more speed from his animal. He hit the ground running, slipping, almost falling, but sliding past Tilman to get to the car. "Mrs. Pegram! Neala!"

Tilman and Butter could hear the hissing of the hot engine as the snow fell on the open fire. Cries of the passengers were faint but audible.

"Hold up, Wagner." On the rail bed above, Pastor Fry got off his horse and slid down to join them. "One of the railroad men from the depot passed me on the way to town, so I came back to help. The bells are already ringing, so people will be here soon. I've assisted in some doctoring. . . ." He was interrupted by renewed cries for help.

"We haven't seen Catherine or Neala or the kids, Paul. Maybe they . . ."

"Don't, Tilman. Pray, man. We'll find them." Pastor Fry stayed by Tilman. Overcome by remorse, he didn't know whether to pray or shout in anger at his God. He had thought his urging of Catherine and Neala to take the luxurious Pullman car was a fitting gift, especially since the telegram had arrived early in the afternoon telling of Neala's win. And what about the children? Pastor Fry tried to move faster but kept slipping in the snow.

A voice came faintly on the wind. "Here . . . over here. We're over here." Sounds of a child's crying came as well, and the men cautiously made their way to where the train rested precariously, broken and torn.

"Neala girl, where are you?" Butter followed Tilman and Paul as they tried to hold up lanterns the men from the depot had brought. During the avalanche the car had tipped onto its side so that the aisle was vertical, and inside the Pullman, darkness made it difficult to see. Snow had continued as if to bury the wreckage of the car. Near the opening several people were sitting, and a few stood near the jumbled remains, looking dazed and unsure of where they were. Between the snow and cold and shock many looked lost.

"Mr. Pegram? Butter? Over here, love."

"Neala?" Butter had tears of fear and joy running down his face, freezing to ice in his beard.

Pastor Fry handed him a handkerchief to wipe his face. "Hold on, Butter. She sounds mighty close."

The three men searched among the torn velvet awnings, and suddenly movement caught Tilman's eye. "She's over there, Butter, to your left. She's waving that bright scarf."

Down on their knees they shoveled snow with their hands, fighting time and cold.

They heard a moan, then a cry, and one of Butter's little ones popped out from under a seat. "Dada."

Butter lifted him up while anxiously looking for his wife.

"Here I am." Neala's pale hand reached for her husband. Butter pulled her up close to him, trying to warm her. Her breathing was shallow and irregular, her eyes dull, her skin pale and moist. "I'm cold . . . where are the children?"

"Shush, Neala love. They're with me, and they're all right. What about you?"

"Cold . . . Janey cut her hand . . . I saw it. Where's Catherine? She took the twins and . . ." Neala shivered violently, the day too much for her. "I haven't heard her, and I've called for a long time." Butter held the children so Neala could see them. She began to cry softly into Butter's coat, holding on as if her life depended on it.

Tilman and Paul carefully pushed their way deeper into the car. The floor they walked on had a short time before been a wall. Now it was a nightmarish cave of broken glass and twisted metal. "Take it easy, Tilman. You're no good to her if you're dead." Light from Paul's lantern revealed that the Pullman had torn open right behind the place where Neala had fallen. Tilman carefully stepped across the split. He heard a noise followed by an angry cry. It was one of the twins. He'd know their crying anywhere. The second twin started hollering as well, loud, angry cries.

"It's the twins! I never knew I'd be so happy to hear them both crying at the same time." Tilman moved toward the crying. "Catherine?" Then he saw Catherine, and she wasn't moving. She was lying on her side with her body protecting the two little ones. Edging around Tilman, Pastor Fry pulled the twins out from their mother's arms. Carefully Tilman lifted his wife. "Catherine. Can you hear me?"

"Look, Tilman." Fry pointed to her forehead and a large discolored lump. A thin line of blood ran down the side of her face. "She's out cold. Probably got hit by something when the car overturned. We've got to get her warm and down to the hospital."

Tilman, his eyes squeezed shut, held Catherine close.

"Tilman! Listen to me!" Paul shouted into Tilman's face until he opened his eyes. "This isn't Sarah, Tilman." He knew Tilman would always blame himself for the death of his first wife, who had died years earlier. "This is Catherine! You hear me? Take the twins. They know you. I'll go get the depot wagon so we can get Catherine down the hill. Hurry."

The twins squalled as their father lay Catherine down and took up the two small screaming babies in his arms. "Wait." Tilman looked for the bag with biscuits and sugar that Catherine always carried for the little ones to use when they needed something to eat. The bag had fallen under an upturned seat. "I've got it." Soon the babies were wrapped in Tilman's heavy coat, safe in their father's arms. Coos and smiles righted their little world, so Tilman held them closely while Paul and several others helped move Catherine into the depot wagon beside the scalded fireman. The next obstacle was the treacherous ride down the slippery trail to the base of Free Gold Hill.

At the station Tilman accepted a woolen blanket offered by the telegrapher, then looped it over his shoulder to form a sling with the twins burrowed against his chest. The telegrapher knotted the ends to secure the sling. Tilman pulled the babies close to him as he climbed into the saddle to follow the wagon down the hill. Butter and Neala and their small ones remained in the depot itself in front of the warm fire, waiting for the others to get there and bring some help for the ones who were not so badly hurt.

The stationmaster made the spartan furnishings of the new depot as comfortable as possible. "I'll make sure it stays warm up here, and we'll get the bunkhouse cooks to boil some coffee. Don't you worry, Sheriff. We'll take care of the others till help gets here from below."

Tilman nodded absently. As he descended into the darkening valley below, an ominous thought seized his mind. Was it the valley of death? A gnawing fear that he might lose Catherine threatened to overwhelm him.

Chapter Thirty-eight

Minna Fry was already preparing the church hall to become a hospital with the help of their friend Pastor Whipple. By chance he had stopped for dinner and the night while on his way to Salida to preach two weddings and a funeral. He'd done some doctoring in the war, and he knew what to do.

Paul Fry prayed steadily as they went down the hill. He prayed for the people on the train, the people down below, and his friend Tilman, who had lost one wife and was now threatened with the loss of a second.

The church fellowship hall had rows of makeshift cots and pallets lining the sides of the building. A potbellied stove was glowing at one end, while at the opposite end chunks of wood blazed in the rock fireplace. The church was near the center of town and could be used for emergencies when needed.

Pastor Whipple helped the town doctor, his memories of being a surgeon's assistant in the War Between the States still strong in his mind. He had started to continue on his journey instead of visiting with Paul and Minna, but he'd felt compelled to stop, ignoring the coming storm, and now he knew there had been a reason. He'd brought a quart of brandy, knowing some of the injured might respond to the stimulant. The women had bandages, boiling water on the stove, and any medicines they'd had at home on hand in case they were needed.

A local boy came running in the door. "I see them. One of the depot wagons is coming in with some people inside. They're coming!"

James Wagner came in with an armload of wood and caught the end of the youngster's chatter.

148

"Did you see my ma, Bob?"

Bob shook his head. "It's snowing again, too hard to make anyone out. I just saw people coming down."

"Ladies?" Pastor Whipple's calm voice echoed through the silent hall. "Let's get some soup into bowls and the hot chocolate poured. This is probably the first group, but the town wagons will be back down shortly as well. All of these folks are going to need warming up and feeding as well as doctoring." His quiet strength filled the room, and soon all were busy.

James grabbed a wool blanket and went to hunt for his family. Down the street he saw Tilman and the twins. "Father! Where is Mother?" He took the two little ones from his father carefully as he looked in the wagon. "Why isn't she with you and the twins? Is that . . ."

Tilman dismounted and dropped the reins. "Here, son. I'll take the twins inside if you'll make sure my horse gets fed and wiped down. Your mother got a bump on the head, and she's here in the depot wagon. You go on, and by the time you get back, they'll have her in a bed here." Tilman tried not to look at James because he knew his son would know what he was feeling. Grief, fear, rage, and prayer were all waging a war in his head.

"But, Father—"

"Not now, son, not now. Please."

Tilman took the sleeping twins and gave them to Minna as he went to help bring Catherine inside to the warmth of the church hall.

"I don't know, Tilman. I think she's just unconscious and in a deep sleep. Hopefully we'll be able to bring her back to us shortly. She just needs to rest." Pastor Whipple watched Tilman as he cautiously chose his words. The man in front of him was hanging on by the slimmest of threads, and Whipple had seen many do the same in the war. He also had seen many men with head injuries like Catherine's. Some woke up tired but fine, and others never woke up at all. He prayed silently that the Lord would give him the correct words when dealing with Tilman. Whipple knew about the man's past from Paul and knew that he was a man who had seen more troubles than most. He moved down the row to look at the burned fireman. He would also have a long road back to wellness.

Tilman sat with Catherine all night and into the early hours of the morning, waiting for movement, any movement. James came for a while, but the grief on his father's face filled him with fear. He tried to touch him but realized his father didn't see him or know he was there. Pastor Fry motioned for James, handed him a blanket, and told him to wrap up by the fire and get some sleep.

Butter and Neala took their children and the twins and went to stay at the hotel as the owner opened all of the empty rooms for the stranded people when they filtered in from the depot. Paul sat with his friend through the night, his Bible on his lap as he talked quietly to his Maker to help his friend and bring Catherine back to her family.

Tilman watched Catherine but saw Sarah, his first wife. He remembered finding her after the Indians had killed her and left her on the ground. He remembered his fury and hate. He remembered the years he had tried to seek revenge and even the score. He remembered his son, Dan, whom he had lost long before the young man was killed.

Early light found Catherine still and unmoving, and Tilman could look no more. "I'll be back, Pastor. I'm going to go sleep an hour or so at the office, and then I'll go see Marshal Early."

Paul Fry nodded and watched his friend go out into the early-morning light.

Chapter Thirty-nine

Outside the church-hall-turned-makeshift-hospital Tilman stood beside his horse at the hitching rail. His left hand grasped the saddle horn, but then he couldn't move. Emptiness filled him. He lowered his head, eyes closed. Prayer wouldn't come. An unbidden thought came instead. *She's never going to wake up.* The church steeple topped by a cross towered above him. When he raised his head, he spoke accusingly with icy resolve. "You took Sarah, and then you took our son Dan. The men who did those murders are dead and buried. Now you're taking Catherine from me. I'll find who did this, and I'm going to make them pay." He swung into the saddle and set off down Main Street at a trot.

Minutes later Tilman strode into the lobby of the Arkansan Hotel. Before he reached the stairs, he heard someone call his name. "Wagner!"

It was Tom Early, sitting alone. The man folded a *Rocky Mountain Gazette* he'd been reading and dropped it to the floor. "I figured you'd come looking for me."

"Let's go talk."

"There's nobody around." Early signaled the desk clerk to bring another pot of coffee. "Why not here?" With an open-handed gesture he motioned for Tilman to sit.

"All right."

Early noted without comment that Tilman, who sat on the edge of the chair across from him, was tense and as dangerous as a coiled sidewinder. He waited until a waitress brought coffee and left their table. "How's Catherine?"

Tilman met Early's eyes. "I doubt she'll live."

151

"I'm sorry to hear that."

Tilman's hands became fists. "I want you to help me find the men who did this."

"Sure, that's what I'm here for."

"I've made some mistakes." Tilman leaned forward, his fury barely controlled. "I fooled around trying to learn to do this sheriff work right, all the while knowing it was not a permanent job. I didn't want to be like Purdy, takin' payoffs. I thought I had time. But I was wrong. I was too soft on the criminals in this Valley, and they ran wild."

Early nodded.

"I want to stir the pot and go smash things. I want people to pay."

"How do you propose to do that?"

"Prosper Charbonneau controlled half this town when I got here. He worked with Bill Ward until Ward got killed. Then Charbonneau saw the writing on the wall. He changed his ways, put up a front, looking like an honest citizen, but he's still doing the same old stuff. It's just under the table. Remember your map? If he doesn't know who's behind these robberies, I'll bet he can tell me who does know."

"Coffee?" Early offered Tilman another cup.

"No."

"And you want me to back you?"

"I do."

Early stared hard at Tilman. "Two lawmen shoot a bunch of robbers, and nobody'll ask any questions. They resisted arrest. Or they tried to escape our custody. That what you're thinking?"

Tilman said nothing.

Early sighed. "I figured Charbonneau's been lifting some of that gold going to the Denver Mint. It's about time we push him around and start the ball rolling. What you got in mind?"

Chapter Forty

Where have you been, Wagner? I've been looking for you the last hour." Butter was huffing and puffing as he got off his horse and faced Tilman.

"Catherine. Is she . . ."

"Come see for yourself, old man. What are you doing? When did you shave last? Catherine isn't going to recognize you."

Tilman pulled his jacket closed. "Lead the way, Butter. We'll talk later."

Mere moments later Tilman reined his horse in, jumped off, and was through the doorway before Butter could get off his mount. Tilman looked for the cot that Catherine had been lying on, and it was there, but it was empty. "Catherine?" He was suddenly afraid. "Where is she?"

Fry motioned from the back corner of the hall, where a hanging blanket formed a small makeshift cubicle. Tilman hurried over to it.

"Tilman?" A weak voice, but a familiar one, called his name.

"Catherine." Tilman knelt down beside the bed as Catherine looked up at him. A bandage covered one side of her head. She smiled to see him, the strain of what had happened showing on her face. "The twins?"

"They're fine, Catherine. You rest. Minna has the boys." Tilman held her hand. "Just get yourself well."

"Tilman, there's something I need to tell you. Something . . ." She closed her eyes, unable to hold them open any longer.

"She'll remember more tomorrow, Tilman." Pastor Whipple stood by his side.

"I'm going after these bandits, Pastor Whipple. You take care of her, please."

"We'll keep a close eye on her."

"I need you to do a favor for me, Pastor."

"What do you need?"

"Just let everyone think . . . Catherine didn't make it. I'm not asking you to lie, but maybe if you can . . ."

"I understand. I'll figure out a way the Lord and I can get along with that. Don't you worry." Whipple watched Tilman leave. Wherever the sheriff was off to, Pastor Whipple was glad Tilman wasn't after him. He did not look like a man who'd turn the other cheek. Not today.

Chapter Forty-one

Butter eased open the door to Tilman's office and peered into the room. Although the shades were drawn, they were of thin material and all but useless for blocking out the bright morning sunlight. In one corner a fully dressed Tilman slept on a cot, snoring. Butter, his heavy boots clunking more loudly on the wooden floors than usual, went from window to window to raise the shades. As he proceeded, light flooded the room. "Two hours, you told me. Wake me up after two hours. It's been two hours, and I'm doing like you said."

"You don't have to shout." Tilman sat upright, swinging his stocking feet to the floor. He was the only man Butter ever knew who could go from dead sleep to wide awake just like that. Jaw working, he ran his tongue across his teeth. He grunted and made a face. "You might at least have some coffee ready."

"The clerk's bringing some."

Tilman pulled his boots on, stretched and yawned widely, and then stood up, shirttails flapping. "Any news about Catherine?"

"I just come from there, and the doctor said she's still the same."

"I hate to get my hopes up."

"Yeah."

The men lapsed into silence while the clerk came in, a pot of coffee in one hand, a cloth-covered basket in the other. The coffee went onto the stove. Butter took the basket and raised the cloth. Tilman shoved his shirttails into his trousers. "That smells good."

"Biscuits stuffed with fried p'taters." Butter set the basket on Tilman's desk and went to the stove. He poured coffee. "Last night and early this morning all the injured were brought down from the wreck site. The engineer and fireman got burned, so we'll see. The fireman got the worst of it. The survivors that weren't hurt got rooms in hotels, and folks opened their homes and took in some."

"You talk to any of 'em?"

"I saw a few of them at the hotel this morning. They say they saw the robbers looking through the express car. Depending on which one you talk to, there were two, three, or maybe six or seven."

"What'd they look like?"

"Couldn't tell. They wore dusters over their clothes. Big hats and bandannas."

Tilman drained his coffee mug. "How many dead?"

"Now, that's curious. They found one man dead, but they don't think he was a passenger. Nobody knows who he is. They found him up the tracks from the wreck, up toward the depot, behind a pile of spoil. Funny thing, though—there was a flower on his chest."

"Suppose he was one of theirs?"

Butter thought for a minute. "Could be."

Tilman combed his hair with his fingers. He took a huge bite from one of the biscuits and chewed thoughtfully. He held out his mug for more coffee, and Butter refilled it.

"Neala and your young'uns safe and sound?"

"Janey got a scratch. Otherwise they're fine."

"Tom Early and I are going to pay a visit to Prosper Charbonneau. While we're doing that, I want you to ride up to the depot to look around and see what you can find. We'll talk later."

"Charbonneau? You got a plan?"

"An idea. Maybe a plan later."

"Hot dang! That's a first."

Butter had slow going up to the depot. The switchback trail was badly rutted from the previous night's rescue traffic. Recovery crews, on a work train sent over from Colorado Springs, were already busy down by the wreck using a crane on a flatcar to move heavy wreckage. The recovery crew boss, an easterner named Giles, had set up his operation in the stationmaster's office. This Giles was a loud and profane man. He lashed at underlings with curses the way a muleskinner used a whip. Against the staccato background tapping of telegrapher's code, there was much hurried coming and going of men around the station.

Glad for an excuse to get away from the commotion and Giles' rough ways, the stationmaster led Butter out across the platform to a small storage shed behind the washhouse. He lifted a latch and pulled open the door. A coffin-sized shipping crate rested on a couple of sawhorses. "Whoever he is, deputy, he's all yours. He wasn't a passenger, for they're all accounted for. The company doesn't want him." He stood aside to let Butter enter. "He's under that."

Butter threw back the ragged, grease-soiled blanket covering the crate. "You packed him in ice?"

"Until somebody claims him, I figured that was best."

"Anything in his pockets?"

"A box of blasting caps. He had a roll of fuse in his hand."

The man lay on a bed of snow and ice. "That's how oysters get shipped in from the coast," the stationmaster noted.

"Don't care for oysters myself," Butter said. The corpse wore a long duster over his clothes and a big bandanna around his neck. A wide-brimmed hat lay on his oddly sunken chest. Flecks of dried blood were caked at his nostrils and the corners of his slack mouth.

The stationmaster lifted a heavy iron fishplate from the floor, a spike rattling loosely in it, and showed it to Butter. "Funny thing, though."

"What's that?"

"We found this lying beside him."

Butter glanced at the iron. "So, what are you sayin'?"

"I walked down the track. There's only one tie plate missing, and that's the one where the rails were torn up in the blast."

Butter took the iron plate and hefted it from hand to hand.

"Unless there's a better explanation, I think we can say this feller with his fuse and caps is the one that set the charge down there."

The stationmaster nodded in agreement. "He put it at a joint where two rails came together to do the most damage."

Butter continued, "When it went off, like a fool, he watched it instead of taking cover. The plate got blowed off and hit him square in the chest. Killed him." Butter dropped the plate onto the floor.

"Can you think of any other way?"

"No, sir, I can't." Butter gazed down at the cold, still face. "Whether he meant to derail the train, or he intended to stop it before it ran off the tracks but cut the fuse too short, we'll never know."

The stationmaster said, "For sure he could have blown up two trains with the charge he used."

Butter covered the dead man's face and asked him, "Who are . . . I mean, who'd you used to be?"

"Some mother's pride and joy," the stationmaster cracked.

"I'll send the undertaker to get him."

"I'd be obliged."

Chapter Forty-two

As soon as Early walked into the sheriff's office, he saw exhaustion heavy on Tilman's shoulders. "Didn't you get any sleep?"

"I did, but there's news. Catherine came to for a short time. I saw her, but then she went under again."

"What'd the doc say?"

"He thinks with rest she'll pull through."

"If you're a prayin' man, you'd best get at it."

Tilman ignored Early's comment. "Doc moved her to a room in the back all by herself. I'm lettin' the news out that she died. I've sent the undertaker out to hang black crepe over our front door."

Early blinked, unsure if he'd heard right.

"Go along with me on this when we get to Charbonneau's."

"Are you sure you know what you're doing, Wagner?"

"I prayed long and hard last night. Not just about my wife but how to catch the criminals who did this to her and the others, and I think I know how we can draw them out."

"Okay. Let's go."

Tilman and Early dismounted in front of Prosper Charbonneau's house. Quickly mounting the short steps and crossing the gallery, Tilman kicked the front door open, shouting for Prosper as he pushed past the housekeeper, Charlene. He made his way through the parlor, followed closely by Tom Early.

From the breakfast room came a shriek. At the sight of the intruders Charlene's helper dropped a serving dish of eggs and ran from the room. Barging in, Tilman found a wide-eyed

159

Prosper at the table with Marcel Devereaux. Clearly the two had been enjoying a late breakfast.

With a vile oath, Tilman grabbed the lapels of Prosper's fancy dressing robe, jerking his face near. "Smiley"—Tilman deliberately used his nickname from the old days—"you were filth crawling out of the sinks when I came to this town, and to my way of thinking you still are! You act the big digs, but you ain't changed." Tilman jerked Prosper from his chair and threw him against the wall. Prosper paled when Tilman drew his pistol and jammed the muzzle hard against Prosper's forehead, forcing his head against the wall. "My wife died this morning because of that train robbery, and I believe you had something to do with it!" Tilman cocked the hammer back. "I intend to kill you right now."

Marcel dared not move for fear the sheriff's anger might be turned on him. The urge to run was strong in him, but he couldn't avert his eyes from what he fully expected to be his uncle's murder.

"W-wait," Prosper gasped. "You're sheriff, and you can't just kill a man out of hand."

A sneering Tilman ripped the badge from his coat and threw it aside. "I'm not anymore. Now I'll kill you as a private citizen."

Prosper looked wildly for help. *The marshal!* "Stop him!"

"Hah!" Early leaned casually in the doorway. "Wagner's made up his mind. He came to kill you right here and now."

"I'm innocent. I had nothing to do with that robbery. I'm sorry your wife died, Wagner, but you have to believe me!"

Early stepped across the room and plucked a roll from a basket on the table. He bit into it, smacked his lips, then pushed the entire roll into his mouth. "Mighty tasty." He swallowed. Turning to Tilman, he reached up and pushed the gun muzzle off Prosper's sweating forehead. "Maybe he's got a point. Now's not the time. It'd dishonor Catherine's memory if you was to blow out his brains. Let's wait and come and take care of him after the funeral."

Tilman holstered his gun. He released Prosper, who fell into his chair. "If you run, I'll come to find you. And when I do, I'll kill you."

In the front of the house, a shaken Charlene sat unmoving in a parlor chair, arms and legs tightly crossed. As the two men walked past, Early tipped his hat. "Ma'am."

Charlene fainted.

Prosper hurried to the liquor cabinet as soon as he heard the front door slam and the sound of horses leaving and splashed Calvados brandy into a tumbler. He tossed it off and then, hands shaking nervously, poured another. When he went back into the breakfast room, Marcel was no longer there. "Marcel?" There was no answer. Prosper frowned. What was his nephew hiding? Prosper went to change clothes and get to his office. He'd better find out what was going on before Wagner came after him for good.

As the two lawmen rode back through the town, Early waited for Tilman to talk. When he didn't, Early broke the silence. "Do you think we did any good?"

"It's too soon to tell. I'll have Butter come up here and keep an eye on Prosper. If he moves, we'll follow him and see what happens."

Tilman returned alone to his office. He found Butter in a cane-bottom side chair tilted back, with his feet up on a corner of Tilman's desk. He was leafing through an old copy of the *Police Gazette*. "What'd you find up there?"

Butter tossed the paper into the wastebasket and placed his hands behind his head, fingers interlaced. "Have a seat, for I got some news. I think we're on to something." By the time he'd finished relating the particulars of the dead body on ice and statements made by the survivors, Butter concluded that, in his opinion, they'd found at least one of the holdup men. "Not that he's in any kind of shape to tell us much. It's a shame he got done for."

Tilman leaned forward in his chair. "That dead man may tell us more than you think. The description of his clothing

matches what people said about the Flower Gang's clothing."
He turned in his chair and looked out the window. "Could it
be the Flower Gang is branching out to robbing trains?"

"It looks that way. One more thing, the stationmaster went
to gather up the mail and such from the wreckage of the express car. He found this a-layin' in the snow beside the cash
box." He tossed a fur-lined black leather glove to Tilman.
"Look on the back."

Tilman caught the glove and turned it over. At the base of
the thumb, embossed in gold leaf, was a small letter *D* in fancy
scrollwork.

Down the hallway the clerks in the repository of deeds
office were startled to hear the shrill ululation of Butter's
rebel yell.

Chapter Forty-three

After a dinner of fried elk steak, boiled potatoes, and biscuits, Deputy marshal Tom Early, toothpick stuck in one corner of his mouth, rested comfortably in the afternoon sun on a bench outside the hotel. That steak was tough, he concluded. His mind shifted to yesterday's disaster up on Free Gold Hill. Early liked to put his facts in order. It was the way he always tried to work, and it seemed to help him think. First off, unless Sheriff Wagner got a lucky break, he'd never find out who was behind the train robbery. Second, Wagner was a tough old hide, and so was his deputy, but they weren't really lawmen, and they were in over their heads. Finally, the railroad was gonna have to bring in some Pinkertons to get to the bottom of the robbery. Those Pinks were good at doing that.

Early chuckled as he thought about the earlier encounter with the Charbonneau fellow. He and Wagner had sure put a scare on him that morning. Prosper was guilty of something, but it wasn't likely he was involved in robbing trains at gunpoint. He'd do his robbing in ways that made him some easy money without the danger. Say, for instance, substituting fake shipping manifests and shorting gold shipments. Early shifted in his chair. Maybe he could get him for something like that.

"Marshal!"

Prosper Charbonneau stood before Early. "Well, speak of the devil, and he appears."

"What?"

"Let it go." Early saw that while Charbonneau had recovered his composure from a few hours before, the man's face was livid. He was in a high state of agitation.

163

"Wagner had no right to accuse me of being in on that train robbery!"

"He tells me you're not exactly the paragon of civic virtue you've set yourself up to be. To put it another way, Wagner holds that a skunk can't change his stripes."

"I'm a victim here too, Marshal. Those robbers stole from me, same as they did the stage companies and old Haw Tabor, and now they wrecked that train and killed poor Mrs. Wagner!"

Early was a man of little patience, and what little he possessed was running out faster than gold dust through a thirsty miner's hands in a saloon. "You? When did you ever get robbed?"

Charbonneau hesitated, for he had told no one, but he quickly continued, "They robbed one of my messengers a while back. Nobody knew I was moving any money like that, and nobody knew I lost it." Charbonneau read doubt in Early's eyes, so his voice trembled with the exasperation of a preacher addressing an unrepentant sinner.

"Yours, huh? Didn't want anybody to know? Why were you hiding it?"

Prosper didn't care for the direction Early's questioning was heading in. "That's none of your business!"

"How do you know it was them that took your money and not some other outfit?"

"Well, I don't exactly have evidence. . . ." He paused and tried to remember what had been nagging him since it happened. "I know. I *do* have evidence."

Early looked interested. "What do you have?"

"There was a flower. When my courier got to Salida, he said that one of the robbers had put a yellow flower in his shirt pocket just before they sent him on his way." Prosper slapped his leg, pleased with himself. "I didn't say anything about it because my daughter thinks I quit doing any business on the other side of the town. You catch my drift?" Prosper stepped closer to Early, emboldened by self-righteousness. "What do you think of that, Early?"

Early stood up, tired of listening to Charbonneau's complaints. "Maybe your messenger got greedy. But wait a minute. Nobody knew, you say?"

"Nobody—that's right."

"Come on, now. You're not the kind to run a little shoestring operation. You've been in business here too long for that. Somebody else had to be in the know."

"Well, my nephew helps out."

"And you trust him, right?"

"Of course. He is the son of my only sister. . . ." Charbonneau turned to leave. "Besides, I've taken him under my wing and taught him a trade and will probably be leaving a big part of my wealth to him. Why would he want to steal from me?"

Early's blood surged. Something was not right here. "Let's you and me pay your nephew a visit. What's his name? Where might he be about now?"

"It's Devereaux. He was sitting at the table when you and Wagner came by earlier. After you and Wagner left my home, Marcel disappeared. Perhaps he has gone to my office here in town."

"Let's go see."

Chapter Forty-four

Climbing the narrow stairs leading to his office above the First Carbonate National Bank, Prosper stopped suddenly. Early, following him, almost ran into him. "What's the matter?"

In a low voice Prosper answered. "The door's open. Marcel never leaves the door open."

Early opened his coat and drew his pistol. Holding it at the ready, he stepped past Charbonneau and, treading quietly, made his way to the landing and partly open door. Throwing the door fully open, Early thrust his gun into the room and followed it into the office. "Don't make a move! U.S. Marshal, and I've got you covered."

Prosper peered into the room. He saw that Early held two men, hands raised, under his pistol. The strangers were caught in the process of ransacking Prosper's beautiful office. "Who are you? What are you doing to my office?" He turned to Early. "I've never seen these men before. They aren't from around here."

The taller of the two, a surly, angular man standing nearly six feet tall, glared at Prosper. "Where's Devereaux?" The other man, shorter but heavily muscled with a vivid red scar from a knife cut below his right eye, stared at Early's gun, saying nothing.

"I thought he was here," Prosper said. "That makes no difference. Why are you looking for him?"

Early barked, "Shut up, Charbonneau. This ain't a tea party." He aimed his pistol at the man who had spoken. "You, what's your name?"

166

"Call me Puncher."

"Your pard?"

"He's Crusher."

Early snorted, the names as good as any. "Okay, Puncher. Be very careful now. Slowly, get your pistol out and place it on that desk."

"I'm not carryin'."

Early stepped to Puncher's side, keeping Crusher in sight. Suddenly he slashed the muzzle of his gun across Puncher's head, crumpling the man into a stunned heap. "Ah-ah," he said, wagging his pistol at Crusher like a schoolteacher admonishing a miscreant student. "Charbonneau, get down there and search that Puncher and see if he was lyin'."

Charbonneau's search quickly produced two hidden guns from Puncher. The man sat up, holding his aching head in his hands, blood streaming between his fingers. Early could see that the stunned man would stay down, at least for a while longer. "Now, Crusher, your turn." Early waved his pistol barrel. "No funny business, or I'll give you another little beauty mark to match that one you already got."

Crusher slowly withdrew a short-barreled revolver from his coat pocket and placed it on the desk. He pulled a second, smaller revolver from his left boot. "That's all."

Early stepped closer to Crusher. "Why do you want Devereaux?"

"He ain't much of a gambler. Lost a pile, and the boss figures he's gonna run. He sent us to collect."

Prosper exclaimed, "Gambling? How much did he lose?"

"I dunno. Boss said for us to get fifteen thousand and then kill him."

Crusher's answer startled Early so much that his breath caught. He was certain he'd found an answer. Prosper's nephew liked to gamble, but he was a loser. He lost and then couldn't cover his markers. And now he'd disappeared. "You, Crusher, collect your friend and get out of this town. If I see either of you again, I'll haul the both of you in as a couple of second-story men. You'll rot in the State Penitentiary over at Cañon City. Git!"

Crusher, unable to believe his luck, didn't say a word. He quickly pulled his pard from the floor and guided him from the room.

"Why'd you let them go?"

"Their kind are a dime a dozen. There's plenty more where they came from." Early moved across the office to a chair under the window overlooking Main Street. Something had caught his eye and nagged at his brain. Draped across the chair was a long, linen duster. In the seat, a wide-brimmed hat lay upside down with a knotted bandanna tossed into the crown. "Look."

Prosper Charbonneau came closer. "Did one of those men leave that?"

Early cussed, cussed louder, cussed himself, cussed the vagaries of his memory, then cussed the kind of man who'd wreck a train for money. He left the room and started down the stairs. "Wagner needs to hear about this."

Prosper hurried to catch up with Early. "Why? What's this got to do with Wagner?"

Early stopped at the boardwalk and looked back over his shoulder at Charbonneau. "That Flower Gang that hit the stage wore dusters and big hats."

The realization stunned Charbonneau. *Marcel!* "I'm coming too!"

Chapter Forty-five

After his uncle had left the breakfast room, a fearful Marcel sneaked away to his own room, grabbed a Gladstone carpetbag, and stuffed it with a couple of changes of clothing and the money he had available. It was only a matter of time until the Flower Gang was discovered.

Skulking out the back door as if afraid to be seen, Marcel dashed to the stable to get his mount.

"Thought you wanted him groomed today, Mr. Devereaux." The old man who worked as a stable hand surprised Marcel. He hadn't seen the man spreading straw in the last stall at the back of the barn.

"Some business came up, and I don't have time. You'll have to groom him later."

"Yes, sir, whatever you say. Need any help with that bag?"

"No, just get the gate." Marcel finished tying the bag behind the saddle and swung himself aboard. He left, taking his time as he rode down to the railroad crossing, waving and speaking to several people along the way. He turned south toward Salida and rode past the edge of town. He turned west, then climbed to the alluvial plain skirting the foot of the mountains before doubling back to ride north to intercept the road to Granite.

Once he got on the road, hard riding would get him to Marie Fleur's by dark. They could make plans to get out while they still could. Since Tilman Wagner had quit the job, how ironic if Peel would now become sheriff. Uncle wouldn't mind that. And he'd owe it all to his nephew, Marcel! He spurred the chestnut on, riding harder than he should. Mountain roads were notorious for patches of water that froze in ruts as soon as the sun went down. He'd ride fast while it was yet daylight. Marcel pushed on. One after another schemes for his and Marie Fleur's escape came to mind, were dissected, improved, discounted, and then discarded. What to do?

Dusk drew deep shadows through the silent hills as the road wound to Granite. Marcel pulled his coat closer and blew on his cold hands. His brown leather gloves were more stylish than warm, and Marcel wished he had been more practical when purchasing them. In his rush to pack he'd looked for his heavier pair but had only found a single glove. Thank goodness it wasn't much farther to Granite.

An elk, unseen in the edge of the woods, dislodged a rock, sending it tumbling down to the roadside, the sound causing Marcel to start. The avalanche of the day before was still fresh in his mind. Was it only yesterday? Probably the blasting powder had caused it. How unfortunate. So much had happened in such a short time. Cooter should have used fewer sticks of explosive and been more careful. Marcel figured Cooter was dead. He'd not seen him since the explosion, and it served him right if he'd killed himself with that blast. But as for Lars, who knew? Lars wasn't bright on the sunniest of days. Oh, well. It was their fault. Anyway, they were expendable.

Chapter Forty-six

A freshly barbered Pastor Paul Fry, hat in hand, stepped from the barbershop on East Main Street. An aura of spicy bay rum aftershave hung about him. Since the train wreck, the town had been upside down, and he hadn't been able to get to the barber, and he had Sunday service coming up. If he didn't grab the moment, he might not have another chance. He turned to study his reflection in the window, turned his head this way and that, and nodded with approval. He raised his hat to his head and placed it carefully, using both hands, so as not to muss the fresh part. He wasn't a vain man, but he also didn't want his congregation to think him scruffy and careless of his appearance.

A sudden thunder of hoofbeats caused Fry to turn about. A rider whipped his horse past him at a dead run, sending clods of dirt flying, heading toward the courthouse. An aproned store clerk crossing the street sprinted to avoid getting run over, his derby hat falling to the street behind him. He shouted a curse and shook a fist at the rider's back.

Hard on the heels of the horseman came another man in a dangerously speeding light runabout. The driver leaned forward on the seat with a grim expression on his face, cracking his whip to urge even more speed from his horse. The derby was crushed under the runabout's narrow wheels. The angry pedestrian scooped up a clod of dirt from the street and flung it at the runabout with more curses. He recovered his ruined hat, shook the dirt off, and tried without luck to reshape it.

The barber, hearing the commotion, came out to stand beside Fry. "What's going on?"

171

Fry shook his head in amazement. "You missed a sight. Prosper Charbonneau was chasing a deputy U.S. marshal!"

"What's the world coming to?" The barber grinned. "Shouldn't that be the other way around?"

"I think I'll go see the sheriff and find out what's happening."

It took only minutes until Fry reached Tilman's office at the courthouse. He stood in the doorway, unsure if he should enter. Marshal Early, holding the embossed glove, was engaged in animated conversation with Sheriff Wagner. Butter Pegram sat perched on a corner of the desk, both feet dangling, listening intently to the exchange. A slump-shouldered Prosper Charbonneau was in a side chair against one wall, eyes vacant, shaking his head. He held an opened silver flask in one hand.

A hand on Fry's shoulder caused an involuntary start.

"Hey, Preacher."

"Holy . . . Peel! Don't you know it's impolite to sneak up on a man like that?"

Seeing the two men at the door, Butter jumped to the floor, his booted feet making a loud thump. "Here's your posse, Sheriff!"

"Posse?" Jim Peel dumped his war bag by the desk. "Somebody better tell me what's going on."

After a handshake greeting, Tilman told both Pastor Fry and Jim Peel that everything they'd found pointed to Marcel Devereaux as part of the gang that had robbed the train.

"And," Charbonneau said—moaned, really—"I regret to say, caused Mrs. Wagner's death."

"What?" Jim stepped back in surprise. He turned to Tilman. "Your wife?"

Tilman sidestepped Peel's question. "We're going to find those people. I'll bring 'em in or kill 'em in the trying."

Butter shouldered into the conversation. "Problem is, old Prosper here says Marcel's run off. We don't know where he's at."

"I do," Peel said. "I mean, I know where he was about two hours ago." The room fell silent.

Tilman's eyes narrowed. "Speak, man. Let's have it."

"I caught the southbound D&RG mail run from Leadville. Up by the flat at Five Elks—you know, where the road runs alongside the railroad tracks? That's where I saw Marcel. He was on a horse, riding north toward Granite and Leadville, and he was laying on his quirt, hard. His saddlebags were full, and he had a Gladstone."

"Probably full of the railroad's money. Maybe mine too, far as that goes." Prosper took another drink from his flask. "How could I have missed the signs?"

"Takes a thief to know one, I'm told, so that's a good question, Charbonneau." Tilman glared at Prosper. "Best quit your bellyaching, and let's get started."

"Is he headed to Marie Fleur's to say good-bye?" Prosper stood, fear and anger making his insides crawl. "If he hurts my baby girl, I'll take care of him myself."

"Prosper, Marie can take care of herself. She's a grown woman with a mind of her own. She'll be safe." Jim spoke with grim assurance. "Besides, I taught her to shoot and ride, and she does a great job with both. Better than a lot of men."

"He ain't got much of a head start." Butter smacked a fist into his palm. "We got him."

"It'll be dark in two hours, and we've done nothing to get ready to ride. Marcel could go to ground anywhere—Fairplay, Vicksburg, or Winfield, we just don't know."

Pastor Fry spoke. "He doesn't know we're coming after him, does he?"

"He left in a hurry, but he probably knows we will be. He just doesn't know when, or how much time he's got."

"Let's steal a march on him." Fry grinned. "If we get on the train, we can get to Granite about the same time he does."

"That won't work," Peel said. "The boys at the station told me there's a freight locomotive derailed at the Wye switch at Nathrop. Won't be any northbound traffic till at least tomorrow sometime. The crane from Pueblo's yard is up here working on the Midland wreck."

Early kicked the wastebasket across the room, sending papers flying.

"Hold it, hold it." Fry raised his hands to quiet the small gathering. "Peel, that southbound you came in on. Is it still at the station here?"

"As far as I know."

"We'll take that and back her all the way up to Granite."

"Wagner, what'll old Andrews say if we steal one of his trains?"

"I'll explain it to him later."

"I don't know. . . ." Butter looked concerned.

Fry wouldn't let go of his idea; he knew it was the best option they had for moving quickly before Marcel disappeared into the mountain wastes. "Slow or not, it'll get us there with fresh horses and do it faster than we can ride it." The former Yankee Army cavalryman was not done. "Why don't we send a telegram to the station at Granite and Leadville? Maybe somebody'll see Marcel."

"What are we waiting for?"

The first autumn stars became visible in the growing evening darkness. A locomotive and tender idled beside Buena Vista's station platform. Behind the tender were a single freight car and a caboose. The cars that had made up the train earlier had been sidetracked. In the red glow from the firebox, the engineer and fireman listened to Early's demand that they keep steam up and be ready to go in an hour. "While you're getting ready, we'll be loading our horses into that freight car."

"I'm going!" Fry shouted, his cavalry blood up.

"I'm going too."

Heads turned. Prosper Charbonneau stood behind Fry, determined to learn the truth about his nephew.

"Huh!" Early snorted. "Suit yourself."

Peel pulled Early and Wagner aside. "We don't know how many we're chasing. A big posse might come in handy if they split up."

"You're right," Tilman said. "Let's get on with it."

At the station the train's engineer nodded soberly. "But if you boys are in a hurry, I have to tell you something." He shifted a quid in his jaw and spat a stream of tobacco juice out the cab window. He wiped his mouth on a shirtsleeve. "This here is a Baldwin engine. She's built for power, not speed. *Slow* don't begin to describe her, especially if we're goin' to be backing all the way."

Butter swung up from the platform into the engine cab and snorted. "Telegrapher says the lines north are down. I bet Marcel cut 'em."

Early cussed again. "He won't get away with it." Turning to the engineer, Early took stock. "This is still the best way to get us and our mounts to Granite. If you can do it, we'll be much obliged."

"Heck, I haven't had this much excitement since a moose calf came walking down the tracks the other day. We were slowing down for a water tank, and right before we hit her, she got off. We'll be ready when you and your men are, Marshal Early. This will be a new one for the books." The engineer went to get his fireman ready to depart.

Chapter Forty-seven

The narrow, river-cut gorge through the mountains opened to reveal the south end of Granite. The twilight deepened, a last faint glow of daylight starkly backlighting the mountain peaks in the west. Marie Fleur's house and the lights of the small town came into sight as Marcel whipped his flagging horse around a bend in the road. How his cousin had lived here as long as she had was beyond Marcel. Granite might have had a chance if Buena Vista hadn't outgrown its boomtown roots. Marie Fleur would surely be glad to be free of this place.

He slowed and walked his horse around to the back of the house to where a paddock enclosed a three-sided shed. Marie's horse nickered in the darkness. He didn't have time for a proper job, but after unsaddling his mount, Marcel hastily grabbed handfuls of straw and rubbed the animal. Rushing, he scooped some grain into a manger and then forked some hay as well.

"Marie Fleur, are you in here?" Marcel peered through the screen and let himself in the back door into the kitchen. "Marie Fleur?"

"I'm coming. What are you doing here?" Marie Fleur came from the front of the house wearing a bright blue embroidered robe. Her eyes were red, and she looked as if she had been crying. "Why do you have your bag?"

"Is Jim here?"

"No. He's gone to Buena Vista to help look for the Flower Gang." She laughed without humor. "If only he knew how close he was." She sank into one of the kitchen chairs and list-lessly waved one hand in the direction of the stove. "There's coffee if you like. There isn't much else. The maid didn't show up today."

"Why did they want Jim to come there?"

"I don't know."

Marcel had never seen his cousin so unresponsive, her eyes so dull. "Have you heard from Lars?"

"No." She turned to face her cousin. "Cooter's dead, isn't he?"

"He must be. We were so busy in the train, I didn't look, but I never saw him again."

"How many others did we hurt?"

"Why do you ask that, Marie Fleur?"

"That avalanche . . . it hit the Pullman car, and I . . ." Her eyes closed.

"You what?"

"Before it hit, I saw Catherine Wagner, and she saw me. She looked at me and called my name. . . ."

"Well, if this makes you feel better, *chérie,* she won't be telling any tales to anyone. I heard Wagner say she died. He blamed my uncle for the robbery and for causing her death."

Marie Fleur wailed, and Marcel could smell brandy on her breath. "We killed her! We left those babies with no mother and a father who won't rest until he finds us." Her hands shook. She leaned against the door frame, her head between her hands.

"Marie Fleur, compose yourself. You've had too much to drink. If Cooter hadn't used too much blasting powder, if the train had had time to stop before running off the track, if the avalanche hadn't come, if we had known Catherine Wagner was on that train . . . so many 'ifs,' and besides, how could we know? It's not our fault." Marcel knelt before her and took her hands from her face, forcing her to look at him. "You knew the chances. Anyway, the avalanche killed her. We didn't."

At least she stopped crying. Maybe, Marcel thought, she'd listen to his plans. "We have to leave tomorrow as soon as it's light enough to see. They came for your father, and when they find out he knows nothing, they will come for us."

Marie wiped away her tears and sniffed. Finally she raised her head.

"Let me fix something to eat while you get packed," Marcel said. "Tomorrow we can go over the pass to Fairplay and from there to Baton Rouge, or maybe New Orleans."

"Why must we leave? How can you be so sure they will know we are responsible? If Catherine is dead, then no one can identify us, can they?"

Marcel reached into his bag and removed his heavy winter glove. "I looked for the mate to this when I decided to come here, and I realized I haven't seen it since the train robbery. I wore it yesterday, and now it's gone."

Marie Fleur was not convinced. "You could have dropped it anywhere."

He shook his head. "You tell me that Jim is in Buena Vista because they know something. Can we take a chance that they did not find the glove? To be safe, let us assume they have it. In that case, they will hang us. . . ." He let the words trail away, desolate in the reality of their predicament.

Marie's hand went to her throat as if she could already feel the roughness of a hangman's noose against her skin. "Oh, Marcel. I always knew your vanity was too great. But a glove, a monogrammed glove, is the end of us. We are going to hang because of your silly vanity." She threw back her head and laughed, the sound a combination of fear and irony. "I'll pack. I need to leave a note for Jim and my father. To tell them not to worry and that I am going to California." She stood. "Yes. I'll tell them I'm tired of the cold and loneliness." She started for her room. "I'll be back in a little while. Make us something to eat, and I'll pack some wine and bread and cheese to travel with."

Marie Fleur went to her room and looked through her clothing, pulling out a couple of riding outfits. She held up a new dress she hadn't worn, a dress she'd need in New Orleans, but laid it aside. She packed some undergarments. The rest she'd leave behind.

She looked for the jewelry her father had given her and put it in a velvet bag along with the money from the earlier robbery. There had not been time for the others to collect their shares. She'd divide it up to put it in several places. She didn't want her cousin to get ideas and leave her stranded and broke somewhere along the way. She managed much better than he did.

A picture of Jim sat on her dresser. She turned it facedown. She didn't want to deal with him yet. Later. Before she left. She took the small picture of her father and put it aside. She would write each of them, but she wasn't sure what she would say. She had not been able to be a mother. She had failed as a wife and a daughter. And, she thought as she wiped a tear spilling down her face, she wasn't a very good robber either. Marie Fleur looked at herself in the mirror and saw only failure.

She found her pen and paper and wrote two short notes, put them into envelopes, and placed one by Jim's picture and one by her father's. She took her small bag into the kitchen and placed it by Marcel's. She gave Marcel a blanket for the sofa, and she went to her room and lay awake as the image of Catherine Wagner's face, the avalanche, the shouts of the passengers, and the sound of the train brakes squealing came back to her until oblivious sleep finally brought her a few moments of escape.

Chapter Forty-eight

The wind picked up again an hour before daylight. Tilman stood in the lurid light of two red collision lanterns on the caboose's rear platform, watching while the train slowly backed into the Granite station yard. Inside, the rest of the posse gathered up their gear, then donned and buttoned heavy coats while Butter finished washing up the tin plates, cups, and utensils that he then dropped into a galvanized bucket of hot rinse water. He'd cooked a breakfast of coffee, eggs and bacon, and gobs of dough fried in bacon grease on the caboose's stove. Butter held that a hot meal helped prepare the men for the work ahead. "I'll leave the rest for you!" he called up to the brakeman riding in the cupola.

The conductor perched on the caboose's lower step. He hung on with one hand while he leaned out and held out his lantern waist high and swung it back and forth, signaling the engineer to stop the train. The engineer acknowledged the signal with a short tug on the whistle cord, the sound soon carried away on the wind. It was earliest dawn, all gray and colorless light. The telegrapher, an Arkansas man known to all as "Pop" Love, stood sleepily on the platform to watch the activity.

It had not been an uneventful night for the men on the train. During the run up to Granite, a small slide had forced them to stop in a deep cut, the track blocked by slumping in the un-consolidated earthen sides. The men brought into play long crowbars to lever several massive boulders off the tracks while pushing away smaller rocks and cobbles. Precious time was lost at that and then still more time inspecting the rails for damage. But at last they were safe in the Granite station yard and could unload the horses to get about their work.

Once again, time was lost when Butter's horse, testy after the unaccustomed confinement on a train, refused to leave the car. When they finally pushed the animal to the door, it balked at the ramp, and Pastor Fry was struck a glancing blow on the thigh when the mare kicked.

He limped painfully out of the car. "I believe the Lord wants me to remain behind today."

An exhausted Butter grumbled in frustration. Finally the five men were all mounted and ready to go.

Fry sat on a station bench, rubbing his leg, breathing a prayer of thanks that it was not broken. The others rode out.

"Look there! I see them. There are two people up there on the far ridge." The night's exhaustion forgotten, an excited Tom Early pointed at the high ground across the river.

Tilman looked in that direction. "I can make out a dark horse and a chestnut. The chestnut must be Marcel's, but who is that with him?"

"It's got to be one of the other gang members."

"We're wasting time guessing. Let's get moving." A bank of clouds gathered above the northern mountains. "We might be in for some more snow by nightfall, and we didn't count on weathering a storm up here."

Early's eyes glowed with battle light, hunting instincts sharpening his every sense. "They're moving slowly. They haven't seen us yet." Tilman spurred ahead, Early close behind with Butter, Peel, and Prosper strung out farther back.

Prosper's easy living had done nothing to prepare him for a mountain pursuit in the saddle. But the man was game. "If that's my nephew, Wagner, who's with him?"

"I can't tell. We're too far away." Tilman set a steady pace, not wanting to wear out the mounts. There was little conversation, for the riders on the distant ridge occupied their every thought. The stage road paralleled the river on their left, climbing and descending the steeply rolling terrain, sometimes offering a view of their quarry, sometimes concealing them.

Tilman was afraid his prey might leave the trail and head up one of the steep gullies leading to higher ground to the right of the road. If he lost them up a gully, he might never catch up. The cold became bone chilling, the wind hard in their faces. Mufflers were tugged up to cover red, chapped faces.

One hour slid into the next, the clouds continuing to spread, blotting out the morning sun, and their horses slowing with fatigue. Almost imperceptibly they gained on the two riders ahead, neither of whom bothered to check their back trail. Tilman was amazed that their quarry were unaware of their pursuers. When he said that to Early, the marshal agreed. "Either that's Marcel and one of his boys, and they're playing us, or they're just innocent folks heading for Leadville, and we've wasted our time."

Butter patted Prosper on the shoulder. "Hold on there, Charbonneau. I got a feeling that's who we're looking for." He spurred up to ride by Tilman and Early. "I'm tired of this. Let's get her done."

They were now close enough to get a good look at the two people dressed in long winter coats and fur caps with ear covers. Who were they? Early shucked his rifle from its saddle scabbard, chambered a round, and fired. He missed. The two riders turned and realized they were being followed. The one in front whipped his horse with a quirt, the animal breaking into a hard run. The other rider drew a pistol and fired several shots at the posse. The distance was too great to hit anything.

"Halt! This is the law!" Early called, but the two riders ignored him.

"Save your breath!" Tilman spurred his tired horse into a hard run. The two riders couldn't outrun Tilman, but neither could he gain on them. He drew his heavy Winchester, rose in his stirrups, and snapped a shot at the rider in the rear. He hit him! The rider jerked at the impact of the slug, nearly toppling from the saddle. His horse slowed, the rider slumped over the animal's neck. The wind carried the wounded rider's voice back to Tilman. "Ride! Go on." The lead rider went over the crest of a hill, dropping from sight, as Tilman came even with the wounded bandit. It was Marcel Devereaux.

Tilman jammed the muzzle of his rifle into Marcel's ear. "Rein up that horse, or you're a dead man!" Early rode up on Marcel's other side. "I got him. Go on, Wagner. This is your show! Go get the other fellow, and I'll take care of this one." He turned to the other riders. "Go with Wagner, and let's finish this now."

Butter, Prosper, and Peel followed Tilman as they crested the hill and saw below a fork in the road, straight ahead leading to Leadville, the right fork to Fairplay. "We should've let Sheriff Hyde know we might be headed in his direction," Butter shouted.

"Who'd have guessed?" Peel spurred past Butter to ride beside Tilman. Patches of snow and ice hid rocks and holes and all manner of treacherous things. The rider increased his lead. Tilman levered a fresh round into his rifle. He'd made one lucky shot. He'd try again or else lose that fellow up ahead. The others were having trouble keeping up with Tilman, their horses about played out. Rising in his stirrups, he tried to draw a bead.

On the wind came the sound of a horse's frightened scream. The men watched as the escaping robber's racing mount struggled and then slipped on a patch of ice, all four legs out from under him. The horse's body slammed into the road, the rider pinned, and then the animal tumbled off the road. The horse and rider parted company. The rider slammed into a rock, his fur cap flew off, and he lay still. The posse reined up, staring in awe at the spill, the rider's mass of long black hair spreading on the snow.

"What in . . . ?" Butter spoke first.

"Marie?" Jim looked in horror, then spurred his horse to the pile in the snow. "Marie!"

A stunned Prosper was unable to speak.

Tilman reined up when Jim dismounted and knelt down by the fallen woman. He held back, trying to sort out what he'd just seen. The robber he'd almost shot was a *woman*.

"Marie. Can't you answer me?" Jim held his wife in his arms, her cap lying beside the rock where she had fallen. One side of her head was bloodied, misshapen, her eye on that side bruised and swelling. He knew that when her horse fell, her head had struck the rock. "Marie?"

Her eyes fluttered open. "Jim. Jim, I didn't mean . . . to kill anyone. It was . . ." She struggled to find words, her voice small, childlike. "It was only a lark, but it got out of hand."

Jim smoothed the hair away from her face as she closed her eyes. Marie Fleur was gone, and the only sound left was the wind. Marie had hated the wind.

Prosper knelt by his daughter's body as Jim Peel, town marshal of Granite, held his wife one last time.

Peel stood. "I'm going to bury her down by the tracks. Not in Granite and not in Buena Vista. This is where she'll lie."

"You can't do that. She's my daughter, and I won't allow it!"

"She's my wife, Charbonneau. You interfere, and I'll bury you beside her."

Tilman and Butter stayed back.

Butter would later say that Prosper Charbonneau seemed to shrink before his eyes. He'd never seen a man so defeated. He looked as if he was a hundred years old.

The Flower Gang was no more. Tilman looked back to where Early and Marcel waited. "Butter, if he lives, I'm going to see Marcel rot in jail."

"Let's go home, Tilman. Catherine is probably up and about, and you need to see her smiling face."

When Tilman turned to look, Butter added, "You need to hear those squalling babies too."

"Hey, Butter."

"Yeah?"

"I found out that *fleur* means *flower*."

"Well, I'll be a son of a gun!"

The two men reined their mounts about and rode back over the hill to find Early and Marcel.

Epilogue

Found on Marie Fleur's dresser upon the return of the posse were two letters. The first was to her father, Prosper Charbonneau.

Cher Papa,

I am too much your daughter, am I not? I should never have gotten involved with Jim, because I always knew we were not intended for each other. I should have stayed in New Orleans and danced the night away or run an elegant club and been who I am. My error was trying to be a lady. I am not.

I have loved the adventure of the chase. I regret that people were hurt and Catherine Wagner was killed. She was a lady, and she treated me as if I were one as well. Unfortunately, things got out of control, and so Marcel and I are leaving.

Do not try to find us. We won't return, and that is best. Build your mansion and live the life of your dreams. I am sorry I gave you no grandchildren, but this is the card I have drawn.

Forgive me,
Your daughter,
Marie Fleur Charbonneau

The second letter was for her husband, town marshal Jim Peel.

Dear Jim,

How do I begin? I do not know the words to try to explain what has led me to where I am now. That would be wrong, and I will not lie to you anymore. I can do that much. You are a fine man. Much better than I ever deserved. My father encouraged this match because he thought you could be led by him and that you would make me a "proper" woman in Colorado society. He tried. I give him that. I fear that I am too much like him, and when I lost our babies and found I couldn't be a mother, something died inside me, and I needed more to fill my empty days. Marcel needed help, and I knew what I was doing and went along for the ride.

I am sorry I hurt you. I am not worth your tears. You are stronger than you think. Live your life well, and think of me only once in a while. I am too vain to want you to forget me forever.

Marie Fleur Charbonneau Peel